Where Deaf People Sing

Alfred John Dalrymple

Revised

Dart

Where Deaf People Sing

Alfred John Dalrymple

Copyright 2003 by Alfred John Dalrymple

* * *

Revised, 2nd edition 2013
Final revision 2015

* * *

ISBN 978-0-692539828
          0692539824

* * *

Published by Dalrymple Books, an imprint of Dart

* * *

BIO

I was born in Portsmouth, N.H....my home base until age eighteen or so...but I also lived in Rhode Island, Hawaii, California, Maine, Connecticut, and Florida.

My father was a navy man...a submariner.

I served in the U.S. Army during the Korean War.

Was at Columbia University. But...have a degree from the Univ. of New Hampshire, and nineteen graduate credits.

In 1967...moved to the Aleutian Islands. Unalaska/ Dutch Harbor. Taught school three years. Had a salmon gear permit...until the Japanese strung out illegal monofilament gill nets, twenty and twenty five miles long. No pink salmon fishing for six years. Then "limited entry" entered, and I couldn't afford to buy a permit for seventy thousand dollars or so, or pay an attorney six thousand a year for renewal.

Fished halibut.

Worked for Unalaska Corporation, and the city of Unalaska, laboring. Then was Parks Manager.

Jigged for cod.

Been to China four times, and to Nepal ten times.

Maybe to Nepal next spring...2016. Then I'll tour Europe, penuriosly, until a rich lady...maybe Miss Universe...takes me in. My hair is mostly brown.

But I didn't tell you much did I?

Title Description

After long oppression...begins the fight for equality.
The oppressor becomes brutal. Some revolutionaries
match the brutality...to be rid of it.

The world calls you terrorist and gives money and
guns to the oppressor.

You laugh and cry at the same time.

You try to love what you hate.

And, with the dignity of existence, you remain
Willing to fight for freedom...against all odds.

* * *

Alf Whitmore has been hired to observe a man who
sells explosives. He follows him to Alaska, China, and
Nepal. In Nepal he sees the face of revolution.

Short description

The word "terrorist" is sometimes given to those
not deserving to be called that. Nepal is another
country hurt by money and guns sent by leaders of
the west.

Corrupted by "caste" and a King who controlled the
military...Nepal entered a revolutionary time which
was forced into a stalemate by western self-service
and ignorance.

Where Deaf People Sing

Act 1 Scene 1

In an office at the Pentagon, a white-haired man, alone, sits at a small inner desk, under a wood sign with black lettering that says "Seven". He gets up and walks to the other desk in the room, this one centered, onto which he places a notebook near a computer having a prominently large screen. Then he goes stage left to the only door.

Done with strength and grace...rather fluid, and having the shoulder roll typical of younger men.

Beside the door is a table made to hold a vase or other small object. On it is an empty glass...which he reaches for and knocks over...so that it falls to the floor, and smashes. He picks up the pieces one by one and sets them on the lower shelf.

He opens the door and looks into the hallway.

Seven-
   Mr. Alf Whitmore...?
Alf (holds forward his hand, and smiles)-
   I'm Alf Whitmore. Are you Mr. Harry Clock?
Seven-
   Yes...but please call me Seven. Where are the other two?
Alf-
   They went down the hall to find the bathrooms.
Seven-
   Come in! I'll leave the door open for them.
   (he walks toward the centered desk)

Mr. Whitmore...Alf...thanks for coming. If you take this job, I'll send you back to the Aleutians, where you came from...and then to China...and Nepal.
Alf-
Does this have to do with terrorism?
Seven-
We expect a bit of it in Dutch Harbor. After that, would your sister go to China? Of course her ex... your friend, Mr. Huxtable...Rob...has an apartment in Shanghai.

Alf's sister, Diane Whitmore Huxtable, now enters.

Alf (to Seven)-
Mr. Clock...this is my sister, Diane.
Diane (holds forward her hand to Seven)-
Rob went to remove a coffee spill...in the foyer.
Seven-
By his choice? A kind man, it seems.

Rob arrives and is introduced. Seven has them sit at the central table.

Seven-
I'm so glad you're here. I'll hire Mr. Whitmore...but we need more help for the China part. It has to do with terrorism...and your job would be to help us locate explosives.
So, here is what I know about you. Alf and Rob... New Hampshire bred...friends more than twenty years. Same jobs, schools, military, also beer, women and jokes. Rob, you're often in Shanghai, at

your apartment...and that's where I'll need you to be.

Diane Whitmore, sister of Alf, once Mrs. Huxtable, which includes several children. Divorced...because that's what happens sometimes. Will you go to China to visit your ex-husband, Rob, to help us locate explosives?

Essentially...that's the job for the two of you.
Diane-

I'll need to travel by boat.
Seven-

Whitmore...yes...I knew your dad. They sent me from Columbia College to the sub base at Groton, to have classes with him. He was a hands-on communications man via ships and subs through World War Two. They said "You want to teach? Watch this man do it!" Well, I was an ex-army ranger, and your dad and I were about the same age. At twenty nine I was younger by six years, but we became close friends. I returned to the military...to the navy...and became a seal, briefly, and an intelligence officer.

Now I'm an old fart...on one more mission. Are you with me, Alf? Do you want the job?
Alf-

Probably. Do I look for explosives? I've been to Shanghai and Nepal...but I assume you know that.
Seven-

Here's the itinerary...as it might begin...and might proceed as planned...but I doubt it. Know what I mean, Alf?
Alf-

I think so...yes.

Diane (interrupting)-

Do you think change is the most constant thing in the universe?

Seven-

I'd say love is. I mean...at the center of things. If you're here, you don't go there...unless you have a need to. I'm thinking of the movement in an atom, and in things even smaller. All things have need.

Am I right, Alf?

Alf-

Sentience resides in all things, in the sense that even existents without "I" maintain themselves.

Surely, love is the basis. But I think my sister is correct to see the necessity of change. Perhaps the Ground allows each unit of itself to go onward both the same as and different from...what it is "now".

Seven-

It's in your book, Alf...which I read.

So...mister Huxtable, what do you think of this?

Rob-

I said those things...last week. But...I didn't get to the Ground of Being.

Seven-

I think we'll all get along fine. So...uh...Diane, we were speaking about...what was it?

Diane-

Our itinerary.

Seven-

Oh, yes...Alf Whitmore is off to Unalaska...Dutch Harbor...with me and my daughter, Heidi. She isn't My daughter. Her dad died when she was four.

(he inserts a disc into the computer, and the

screen shows a man's face)

This is Mr. Mosawi. I say Mr. only to highlight his firm place as a terrorist. He sells explosives...and will bring some into Dutch. Alf, you and Heidi must determine how it arrives. Most likely it will come by a container ship. Sure! The dynamite will be in a van, and they'll drive it off. And you need to find out what their target is.

Alf-

Maybe they want to blow the fuel dock and its storage tanks. Sorry! I shouldn't interrupt.

Seven-

We suspect that. Also, we think Mosawi is a seller only. Other terrorists will be waiting.

Let's get on to China!

(he moves the disc's picture ahead, to show Mosawi with another man, this one younger, about twenty, and of a softer, more smiley aspect)

This young man is Nepali. See the rounder face. And although he's smiling, his mouth has a firmer base of character.

Raju Lamichane...he owns a Nepali restaurant in Shanghai.

Rob...you'll get an apartment. Diane, you'll be visiting him, your ex-husband. Then Alf will arrive. The three of you go eat at that place. And, likely, Mosawi will be there. Excuse me! Mr. Mosawi.

Diane (points at the screen)-

Was Raju born in Nepal?

Seven-

Yes. He was raised there, until age eight...in a mountain village. Not High...about five thousand feet. Of a low-caste Hindu family...landless and with pennies...eating what they grow, or carrying it to market. Did I say low-caste?

Rob-

I read...they don't own land, but often borrow money from those who do...in order to keep from starving. Alf would know about that.

Seven (glances at Alf)-

Yes...the land is owned by high-caste elite, living in the urban centers, most of them in Kathmandu.

Diane-

How did Raju get to China, and come to own a restaurant?

Seven-

At age eight he was brought to New York by a rich American...who intended to extend his education. Well...time passed. At age twenty he met Mosawi at Columbia University. We know that...but can only guess about the words that went between them. I assume Raju has the same goals as most Nepali rebels...to rid the Hindu system of caste, and end centuries of oppression.

Anyway, the rich American died and left Raju a couple hundred thousand dollars...and a restaurant in Shanghai.

Alf-

Will Raju soon go to Nepal?

Seven-

After Mosawi finishes in China...that seller is off to Nepal. He has his ticket...and so does Raju.

(he shows another picture. There is a red-haired girl, apparently in her twenties or early thirties)

Alf-

  Holy smacks...! The sun is up! I can feel the heat!

Seven (sighs)-

  This is Heidi Hoadley. I think of her in a fatherly
way. Her dad died when she was four. And I'm
seventy five.

  Call me Seven. My name is Harry Clock, but please
don't call me Mr. Clock.

Diane-

  Mr. Seven. I mean...Seven...will Heidi Hoadley go
with my brother to Unalaska...Dutch Harbor?

Seven-

  Yes...and later they'll arrive in Shanghai as though
married. After that...it'll be off to Kathmandu, for
the buggers. Ah!...to be a kid again.

Rob-

  This happens if Mosawi is only a seller. If he uses
explosives, he'll die in Unalaska or be arrested?

Seven-

  Probably.

Rob-

  In any case...will you pay my way to Shanghai?

Seven-

  Yes...you would have a ticket today.

Diane-

  Can I go by boat? I don't like to fly. And when
would I get my ticket?

Seven-

  Tomorrow. I'll send you a confirmation number.

Act 1 Scene 2

There is a long bar, with stools, but Alf, Rob and
Diane go to a table, which is one of a couple dozen.
The place is well-lit, but the woods are dark and the
windows small and about ten feet above the floor.
　Resting on the bar-wall mirrors is a six feet long,
reddish piece of wood with black lettering showing
the name of the place: Seven.

Alf (as they sit)-
　Nah! The government would be against it.
Diane-
　He seems to be a kind old fart. Wouldn't it weigh
　on his conscience, to think how often a man comes
　screaming across the floor with a beer bottle and
　smashes it against someone's head?
Rob-
　Could be a woman.
Diane-
　To get hit?
Rob-
　To come screaming across the floor.
Alf-
　I feel that I'm on the road again...in a military way.
　Fate will be driving, but she'll take me to bridges I'll
　be ordered to cross.
Rob-
　Seven won't be watching you all the time, Alf.
Alf (to both Diane and Rob)-
　At the bridge we just came to...we are free to

choose. Do you want the job?

Diane-

    Alf...I'll go to Shanghai. But the choice is easier for me...I'll have a small part. And Rob.

Alf-

    You can be blown up...in small parts.

Rob-

    What do you say, Alf? If you take it...I'll take it. Yes or no...it's your call, my friend.

Alf-

    All right! I'll tell you of my gut reaction to it.

A waitress comes toward their table. She has a black mini-skirt and white blouse. Her hair is black, and her face very white, from powdering.

Alf (to Diane)-

    I'm saying this to Rob.

    (speaks to Rob)

    Say...what do you think of her? In a split instant, she's in my hall of fame.

Rob-

    That was a lickety split decision.

Alf-

    No! There's something about her which is above your drivel.

Rob-

    Anyone above my drivel is beneath my contempt. Alf, I doubt that she is.

Diane-

    She's wearing a wig.

Now, also, the bartender comes around toward them. He seems a bit old for the job, and yet has a large glob of flaming red hair.

Waitress-
    Can I help you?
    (she looks at Diane)
    I must ask...where did you get that suede coat?
Diane (reaches for her purse)-
    In Boston...as we drove through. Here's the
    address and phone number.
Alf-
    And yet...she was looking at me first.
Rob-
    Maybe she thinks you need a drink.
Waitress (to Alf)-
    Would you like to order, sir?
Alf-
    Why did you ask me...first? He has white hairs in
    his beard. I don't have any.
Waitress-
    You have no beard. Can I ask you a question?
Alf-
    Yes.
Waitress-
    What is Shangrila?
Alf (with a serious demeanor)-
    You ask as though you mean it...and want me to
    answer seriously. Well, it could be the place I seek
    in my dreams...and can't find it. I lost my ticket, or
    the location of the departure station. Or...as I go
    down the road, I begin to drift, and forget what I

was looking for.

The bartender arrives, but only stands, listening.

Waitress-
   Answer it! What is Shangrila?
Bartender-
   And...could it be here?
Alf-
   It can be here for those who are properly just...
   attending to actions only...and even if hating the
   act...able to love the center of the one who acted.
Rob-
   How many of us could get there, Alf?
Bartender-
   What are you between thoughts?
Alf-
   Good point. Being "loving only" between thoughts,
   ought to be acknowledged when we're not there.
Rob-
   To be "loving only" even as we think? That seems
   like a resting place beyond most of us.
Alf-
   I'll give a more useable answer. Shangrila...is
   here for lovers. That's a happy place set up, as
   permanent and separate....yet allowing the going in
   and out of what surrounds. And they see the comic
   in this divinity. Their "I" can laugh in sad disbelief,
   and chuckle as a tear rolls down. Well, not chuckle.
   How do you laugh and cry at the same time?
Bartender (looks at Rob)-
   And you?

Rob-

    I could do that. Or get drunk in anticipation. Who needs a resting place?

Bartender-

    Well...if you don't, maybe you're already in one.
    (looks at Diane)
    Is he? You ought to know.

Diane-

    He could be. Why did you say that? "I ought to know". Do I know you?

Waitress (to the bartender)-

    Dad...one minute, please.
    (again she looks at Alf)
    What's the difference between the tragic and the very sad?

Bartender-

    Daughter...do you mean the tragic and the comic?

Waitress-

    No! It would take too long to answer that.

Diane-

    I know both of you!

Bartender (smiles)-

    That's because she called me Dad.

Waitress (Heidi Hoadley)-

    What's the difference between the tragic and the very sad? Remember...we'll be working together.

Alf-

    How would I know? I think...tragedy is allowed by light in the darkness...and so...can't exist without hope which is crushed but can't be lost. Mountains crumble, galaxies collide...but there is no tragedy unless the "I" is hurt and a dream seems to have

been lost but it hasn't, in the lingering of it.
Heidi-

 If this tart thinks you're fruitless...you won't be
hired, Mr. Alfred.
Diane-

 Alf...in your books...you say awareness resides in
all things. Even atoms and their parts self-maintain.
But isn't the "I" inside them, too? Or else, when you
split them...why do they blow up ten square miles
when they scream?
Heidi-

 You're hired, Diane. I don't know about your
brother.
Seven-

 I'll do the hiring, daughter.
Heidi (to Alf)-

 What of the words "The chosen people"?
Seven-

 You don't need to ask about that.
Heidi (to Alf)-

 There's a beach filled with a hundred billion grains
Of sand. When you look at it...what do you see?
Alf-

 A sandy beach?
Heidi-

 Could each grain be a planet or a star or a galaxy?
Think about it. Now what do you see?
Alf-

 That each grain could be a universe.
Seven-

 Heidi...take off the wig!

She takes it off, and reveals hair of a strawberry hue worn, knotted, at the top of her head. Quickly, she loosens it, and tumbles it down around her shoulders. Then she uses a rubber band to assemble it into a singleness.

The old man takes off his glob of fiery red hair.

Seven (to Heidi)-
You're not yourself today. What's the problem?
Heidi (looks downward, shyly)-
Nothing! Let me continue...please!
Seven-
The tenor of this time is "I am better than you!" We ought not to confine it to a specific religion.
That we're all the same inside...all equal at the center...is what this group agrees to.
Alf (to Heidi)-
I think...justice is blindfolded, so she can attend to actions only. Knowing of the innocence within, she treats every person equally.
Diane-
Do we refer all this back to her question about the beach? If we can be humble, it's easier to see God in every grain of sand?
Rob-
Because we agreed to equality...Mr. Seven has suggested we ditch this line of questioning.
Seven-
Well said.
Alf-
And so, Rob...my friend...it's been awhile since we tipped a mug, together. Heidi...I can tell you have a

warm heart. Would you arrange a beer delivery?
Heidi-
    I'm not finished! At least your sister is smart. Now,
what is the difference between the terrorist and the
revolutionary?
Seven-
    No! In today's world...terrorist can be description
of a religious fundamentalist...or a Neo-Nazi racist.
It can be used for a group of murdering thieves who
pretend to be rebels. Refer him to Nepal...Heidi.
That's where the question will arise; and where the
people have been oppressed for centuries.
Alf-
    Is that the way to say it? The revolutionary is
fighting for equality...after having been oppressed.
Rob-
    But...once fighting begins, isn't it sometimes hard
to know who is which?
Alf-
    Sure! The revolutionary must match the brutality
of the oppressor's effort to beat him down.
Seven-
    Good, Alf. In Nepal, if the Hindu system has been
oppressive for centuries, one way of terrorism is at
the center of all activity...in caste. It has muddied
the feet at the bottom...and powered parliament
and the king. I speak of privilege and wealth.
Alf-
    As the revolutionary acts...the privileged become
brutal. Soon...all involved use excessive force.
Rob-
    The revolutionary will become brutal. Sure! But

what of those who are brutal according to the
nature of murderers and heartless thieves?

Diane-

The revolt can lose the confidence of the people.
Every revolution needs an outstanding leader, in
case it flounders.

Alf-

That must be true. But...Nepal's terrain has few
roads. Living two hundred miles apart could seem
much farther. Perhaps this revolution will have
dozens of separate armed groups. Hopefully, they'll
be under control.

Seven-

Yes...the geography will impair cohesion. It will be
difficult to have unity.

Diane (to Seven and Heidi)-

Why did you dress that way, then soon let us know
your identity?

Seven-

We intended to be incognito, but I changed my
mind. I don't like trying to fool people I know, once
the attempt begins.

Heidi-

He has huge false teeth. Show 'em...Dad.

Seven-

No! This is serious business. So...will you join us?

Alf-

Yes...I'm for it! I thought I said that yesterday.

Rob-

I'll be available...in Shanghai.

Diane-

Yes, if there's a boat leaving soon.

Seven-

I'm happy you're all in. My daughter Heidi...
(puts his arm around her shoulders)
She's Heidi Hoadley. Alf...if you call her Heidi Ho,
you'll be down the road. But...circle back to her,
she didn't mean it.

Heidi-

Why are you talking this way, Dad? You're trying
to embarrass me.

Seven-

You've been a bit snippy. Something's bothering
you, and I think I know what.

Heidi (pointing at Alf)-

He's got to know who the boss is.

Seven-

I think he knows...and so do you. If you two climb
a mountain...you can lead the way up...and he can
be directly under you.

Act 1 Scene 3

(Unalaska/Dutch Harbor)

In the cafeteria of an all-purpose store, Alf sits at a table beside a row of large windows. You can see mountains in the distance, west, and one nearby, a quarter mile to the north. And the sea is at hand...a strip of bay out from the window a couple hundred yards.

Heidi enters. She comes to the table next to Alf and looks through the window.

Heidi-
    Hello Alf...let's cut the chatter. Have you seen Mosawi? I'm to have dinner with him, this evening. I said I'd be at the Grand Aleutian Hotel at six thirty and stay until eight because I have an appointment with mister Alfred Whitmore, my climbing partner. I told him we'll be going to Shanghai to buy ropes and parkas for a climb of Everest. So, I mentioned we'd be in Nepal soon, and I might be climbing, but mainly I'm the expedition secretary and nurse.
Alf-
    Did you tell him you're nursing a bit of hate for your partner, so you need to sit at a different table?
    Oh, cut the chatter, Alf!
    Have I seen Mosawi? No!
    You can look at me!
Heidi (looks at him, and then down at her table)-
    You're nothing to me! Remember that!

Alf-

How was your flight in?

Heidi (comes to him, and sits, but again looks down)-

I thought the jet was crashing into that mountain.
(points to the one beyond her right shoulder)
Does the wind always blow gale force? At the last
minute...the plane's nose was pushed toward the
water at the end of the runway.
(she looks up at him)
Everyone screamed. And Mosawi was scared into
himself. He just turned white....not only his face but
his knuckles, too, holding his knees. I sat with him.

Alf-

What did he say?

Heidi-

Aaaagh! Oooo! And then he said "There is no other
God but Allah!"

Alf-

No!...I mean what did he say during the flight?

Heidi-

I know what you mean! He said nothing...hardly.
He slept almost all the way. But I began to chatter,
to force him to notice me. So, he looked me over
and, without expression, invited me to dinner...all
the while talking to the seat in front of himself. He
said "I'm free 'til six in the morning...but you can
sleep longer. Just get out by ten."

Alf-

I'll be at the hotel entry. If you're not out...by five
after eight...my rescue will begin. Did you ever see
a man used as a piton, and pounded into a wall
crack?

How's that for chatter?

Heidi-

   Dumb! I'm nothing to you...and you're nothing to
me! You must remember that! If he comes here,
don't hardly look at me. What are you looking at?

Alf (he laughs)-

   You hair! After I looked at your, you know...but,
why are you making such a thing of it? We're not
attracted to each other. It's obvious.

Heidi-

   Then don't joke about pitons. I don't believe in
soul mates.

Alf-

   Sure! It's ridiculous. If I had such a thing, all I
would need to do is go about my business...and
there she'd be, after awhile...right in my face.

Heidi-

   That's dumb! You'd have to wonder about every
girl who went by.

Alf-

   Only if she got in my face. Here comes Mosawi. Go
to the ladies room, sweetheart!...so I can talk with
him for a minute.

Heidi (gets up, and takes one step)-

   I'll fire you! And don't call me that!

Alf-

   I didn't mean it. I wasn't trying to be bossy. I can
get to talk with him more openly if you're not here.
   (she departs)

Enter Mosawi, who comes to the same table Heidi
was at. Then he looks through the window...and over

his shoulder...north...toward the airport and the adjacent mountain.

Alf (speaks toward Mosawi)-
Rainy...windy day. This island is seventy miles long, and is filled with mountains of the size you can see on the other side of the bay. That's west, straight through the window. Behind you, north, is the airport runway...and Ballyhoo Mountain. Of course, we are on the Bering Sea.

Mosawi continues to look through the window.

Alf-
My name is Alf Whitmore. I'm a partner of Heidi Hoadley. We'll be off to Shanghai to buy ropes for an Everest attempt. Kathmandu is the base, but the climb will be from the north...Tibet-China...because there's a bit of danger in Nepal. A revolution rages.
Say...are you from Pakistan?

Mosawi jerks his head toward Al, and glares at him.

Alf-
What do you think of 911?
To be murderous and think you're not...is insanity easily produced by institutional religion. Thus the Crusades. It works both ways. What do you think of the words "The chosen people"? Next year we increase our aid to Israel to a few billion. We yelled it out, from Congress, probably thinking to rub the face of terrorism.

If I were a moslem I'd find it unfair...to say the innocent people of Palestine are not worth much help. Don't you think Israel ought to get their settlements out of Palestine?

Mosawi turns very pale, although his eyes never leave Alf. His mouth opens wide.

Alf-
     Look at you! You're a Pakistani?...but you're not a terrorist.
Mosawi (waves his hands in a crisscrossing manner)-
     No!
Alf-
     Did you ever have flight training? I ask it, rudely, to make a point.
     Christians have had missionaries for centuries... often thinking they're better than you. A high-caste Hindu might spit at a person of lower caste...now assuming it's you...in order to clear the air of your foul presence. Also, they wouldn't take water from you, it having been defiled by contact with a piece of shit.
     Do you think I'm the devil? That's not funny!

Mosawi stands and fastens a button of his coat. He continues to glare at Alf.
     Now Heidi returns. She nods her head at Mosawi, and sits at Alf's table.

Alf-
     I was being rude to Mr. Mosawi...by suggesting

that more slaughters, of body and mind, have been committed in the name of God than any other.

God's name ought not to be defiled so. But what do I know? Will love protect both my humility and my certainty...when I define terrorism as something to hate?

Mosawi-

Yes! You must learn to humble yourself! You are nothing!

Alf-

Thanks! You, too!

Heidi-

I'm ignorant about Unalaska. Where are the fuel docks, Mr. Whitmore? And don't they also call this Dutch Harbor?

Mosawi sits.

Alf (points north)-

If you return to the airport...and you can see it, Heidi, if you turn your head...and from there look directly east, the dock is off the end of the runway, about five hundred yards. Most of its fuel tanks are beyond it, as you continue along the shore and go around the corner. So, it would be an easy target for a terrorist. Of course...there are none here.

(he speaks over her shoulder, to Mosawi)

Have I been lacking in humility? Sometimes I look up at the stars, to remind myself we're all made of that stuff. It maintains itself through allowed laws. Then "I" appears...and often forgets to love.

It was nice to meet you. Heidi said she's dining

with you at the hotel...until eight. Maybe she can dog you for information about Afghanistan. I'd like to go there one day. I'll be waiting for Heidi in the foyer, at eight. I get up at seven.

Heidi kicks Alf in the shin. Then she gets up.

Heidi-
Thank you for the coffee, Mr. Whitmore. I'll see briefly, this evening.
Alf-
Good afternoon to you...Miss Hoadley.

After Heidi departs, so does Mosawi...without a word or a glance toward Alf.
An old lady has been cleaning table tops, bending low to the surfaces, wielding a large rag in each hand. As Alf finishes his coffee, she arrives at the next table.

Old lady-
Hello, Alf. Yes, Mosawi has met two men.
Alf-
Mr. Clock...Seven...how are you?
Seven-
Doing well, thanks. Two men came to Mosawi's room at the hotel. They said the explosives are here, already in place...which made him angry that his mail was picked up before he arrived. Then they paid him. He said he leaves the day after tomorrow, on the eleventh.
I heard whispering...and some clunking sounds.

Which means, of course, they found the bug.
Alf-

 Heidi is having dinner at the hotel with Mosawi.
Seven-

 No! I just cancelled that. The two other men will
be there...and the entirety becomes dangerous. So,
I'll go...and bug their table.

 (looks at his watch)

 The other bug...I'll put inside sticky bread dough.
Alf-

 Where is Heidi staying, Mr. Clock? Seven.
Seven-

 At Carl's Hotel...across the bridge. It's not far
from Marilyn's Hair Salon, where I just got a trim.

 So...now we're on a smaller island. Oh...wait! You
live here. Tell me about it!
Alf-

 Yes, a separate island...and the big island it's
bridged to is seventy miles long. Seven...I have a
friend who is eighty, who takes a folic acid tablet.
Seven-

 And so...?
Alf-

 He has difficulty remembering things, but is alert,
otherwise. Oh...there's a bit of fading awareness.
Sometimes he leaves his stove on and the water
boils away, and things like that.
Seven-

 I don't have that problem. What is it we were
talking about?
Alf-

 Mosawi is departing in two days.

Seven-

I know. I just told you that. You and Heidi will be on the same jet. I'll get that news to Mosawi, so he won't think you're following him.

Alf-

Oh! I almost forgot! I've had email contact with my sister, Diane, and my pal, Rob. He's in China.

Seven-

And your sister is on a boat. I almost did forget.

Alf (reaches into his pocket)-

She was...on a boat. Let me read her note. She Says "It's me, in Tokyo. We pounded through a Storm, and I'm yet tossing my insides. Didn't think I'd ever say this, but I'll be taking a jet from here.

Maybe it was fate that got me puking, and led me to the airways...so I can face death instead of that other stuff.

Say "Hello" to Rob, in Shanghai...and to Seven and Heidi and Jane".

Seven-

Who is Jane?

Alf-

My sister, in Las Vegas. I gave you her address, in case I die on this mission. Of course...Heidi knows who to contact if you slip away. Shoot! A tough old fart like you will live to be ninety-five.

Seven-

What was the question?

Alf-

Did you and my Dad...ever get drunk together?

Seven-

A lot of times, son.

Act 1 Scene 4

Alf and Heidi have climbed to a level resting place on the side of Mt. Newhall. Heidi...first arrived...lays on it, face down. She has a dark brown wig, with hair flowing to the mid of her back. Now she takes off the wig, loosens her red hair, and puts a rubber band around it at the nape of her neck.

Alf-
   I want to rest, too...maybe.
Heidi-
   Stay where you are...beneath me! Keep me safe!
Alf (comes up high enough to lean against her)-
   We're almost to the top...another hundred feet of this steep part, and then some easy walking for a couple minutes. Sit up! Or I'll lay on you.
Heidi-
   No! Alf...we're probably being observed, from down there.
Alf-
   More likely from above. Someone up there was laughing at your disguise. Now they're crying at your reason for hogging the resting place.
   It's all right! Joy weeps!
Heidi-
   Oh, Alf, does fate laugh and cry? Get your hand off my back! Don't lean on me! Where is the runway?
Alf (sits partly on her back...then points west)-
   It's directly across the bay from us. Just south of Mt. Swanson.

Heidi-

But, Alf, it's called Mt. Ballyhoo. They say Jack
London named it.

Alf-

Ballyhoo means much ado about nothing. It's an
insult! So...I changed it.

Heidi-

Who is Swanson?

Alf-

Henry. He was a fox farmer, and trapper...trader,
and fisherman. He piloted ships during the Second
World War, throughout the Aleutians...as a captain
in the U.S. Army.

(he leans against her)

In the First World War he was a youth in the navy,
on a cruiser. He said that one day he was standing
amidships, by himself, leaning against a railing, and
he saw a torpedo coming. It arrived...and he was
looking almost straight down at it. Then a huge
swell lifted the ship. The torpedo went underneath.

I wonder if the captain of the submarine saw him?

Heidi (rolls onto her back)-

You lie!

Alf (looks at his watch)-

It seems strange that you're having lunch with
Mosawi. Why would he ask you? At the cafeteria,
you didn't hardly speak to him...then you cancelled
the dinner date.

Heidi-

Maybe I winked at him, Alf. So...I'll try to get more
information. For instance...he might be called on
his cell phone. A note could be delivered.

Alf-

   He's leaving tomorrow. Seven and his boys have located the explosives, and are waiting to catch Mosawi's customers trying to use it. What's left for us to do, except pack and be ready to depart.

Heidi-

   Seven is not sure they found all the explosives. Also, there could be other targets.

Alf-

   Heidi, take care! At lunch, Mosawi can speak to a special burger, and your pants will blow off. It's no laughing matter!

Heidi (laughs)-

   In the main dining room? I'm above your drivel.

Alf-

   And so...beneath my contempt. I said that a few days ago.

Heidi-

   No! Your pal, Rob, said it.

Alf (he lays on her, almost fully)-

   He stole it from me. And now...you're beneath my body and my soul. Also...

Heidi (pushes him slightly away)-

   We're being watched, I said! Tell me more about Henry Swanson. I...

   (she stares at the uphill edge of his shoulder)

   Ahh! No! Alf!

   (firmly grasps his shoulders and pulls him to her)

   Stop! Aahh!

Alf-

   How wonderful! And so sudden. All I did was think about kissing you.

Heidi (she points down the hill)-

    That big rock flew past! It would have killed you.

    Let's go! I've had enough of your tomfoolery.

Alf-

    Down?

Heidi-

    Up!

Alf-

    I can identify whatever you need to know, from
here.

Heidi-

    Let's go to the top, Alf. We have time. And you can
climb under me, always, in case I begin to slide.

At the top...as they cover the final steps, Alf has
taken Heidi along the ridge, away from the edge. Now
they sit where they can get the best view downward
and around.

Heidi-

    The airstrip is almost straight across from us.
That's west? Mt. Swanson is at the north edge of it.
And down here...(points to the left)...is the town, I
mean the city of Unalaska. Once upon a time...it
was a bit of a letdown, after the ballyhoo...to Jack
London. In your opinion.

Alf (points down to the town)-

    Here's the school, and Whittern. Gregory and
Svarney. Farther along the beach is Marilyn's Hair
Salon...she's a Krukoff McCracken. Then Nick
Lekanoff, and Ben and Suzi Golodoff. Away from the
water is Sophia Sherebernikoff. I only named a few.

Heidi-

Why did you do it so abruptly? Are you angry?

Alf-

Will you ever care about those names?

Heidi-

I'd like to know all your friends, Alf. But...you're right...let me attend to the job. The attacks will be across from us, at those oil tanks, or at the runway. Where is the main fuel dock?

Alf-

Out of our sight...between the tanks and the runway. Just around that corner. When the jets take off this way, they're not far from it.

Heidi-

Look at the weather. Clouds are forming below. Also, behind us they're thick, Alf. Will it rain?

Alf-

Later, maybe. The sun is coming through quite a lot of moisture. See the round rainbow...behind us? It's sitting on the cloud, just a bit below us.

Heidi-

The rainbow is a circle. Look...Alf...that's us in it.

Alf-

Yes, we're inside it.

Heidi (leans against him and holds his arm)-

It's blue inside it! Clear blue sky. But...why don't we see grass? Did we die? Do we walk through it?

Alf-

The sun is behind us, now, and has made a circle, a rainbow on the cloud...and we're in it.

Heidi-

Why, Alf? Do we go to heaven together...now?

Alf (he takes her hand)-

    No! Walk along the ridge with me, a few feet.

    See? We go where it goes. It's just a rainbow...and
the sun is behind us, centering us within it.

Heidi-

    Oh, well. I guess I'm rather ignorant.

Alf-

    I've seen them before. I know how you feel, Heidi.
Maybe this is a good time to put my anger aside,
and tell you that I sort of...uh...like you. Why would
I go into the afterlife with you, if I didn't?

Heidi-

    But it caught in your throat...like a rainy day lie!
Would you go into the afterlife with someone you
sort of like? Look! We're yet in that damn thing! If
this is fate...kiss my patootie! And don't touch me!

Alf-

    Well...same here! And frig the rainbow!

    An explosion now occurs, and they see a black
cloud. It billows strongly into the sky, at the area of
the fuel dock.

Heidi-

    Dammit, Alf, they struck!

    (she steps toward the way they came, then turns
and waits for him)

    They walk along the ridge.

Alf-

    I'll go first...and descend at the fastest speed

safety allows. And I'll be just under you, in the bad places, to catch you if you fall. Use your stick on the upside of the hill, above you...as I said, earlier.

Heidi's cell phone rings.

Heidi (looks at Alf as she speaks)-
Hello...Dad. Oh, good! Be careful! All right. Alf and I are on Mt. Newhall. You saw us? Yes! I'll see you, later. Don't forget your reading glasses!
What?
Yes. All right!
(she puts away the phone)
Alf...they caught two terrorists just as the small explosion happened, and prevented a more serious blast. But more operatives are here, so he'll be busy. We leave tomorrow, he said.

Act 1 Scene 5

As Alf enters the terminal he has his leather jacket
over his head to shield him from the wind and rain.
　Once inside, he goes to the counter.
　Heidi is there...looking at her ticket. When she sees
him, she steps away.

Alf (to the lady at the counter)-
　Lavera...good morning to you!
Lavera-
　Mr. Whitmore. I have your boarding pass...all the
　way to Seattle. Do you have bags to check?

　Now enters a demanding voice from behind Alf. It
belongs to a dark-haired, heavy man, apparently a
moslem...with a close-trimmed beard.
　There is a second man of similar appearance,
except that he's thinner and shorter.

Heavy man-
　Pardon me! Will you wait on me, please!
Lavera-
　Here's your ticket, Mr. Whitmore. You have a good
　time...wherever you're going.
Alf-
　Thanks, Lavera. I'll be...
Heavy man-
　Please! I need to be helped! I insist!
Lavera-
　You can wait a second. (she smiles at Alf)

Just beyond the end of the counter, Alf turns right, into the waiting area. He goes to the windows, facing the runway.

(a man appears beside him)

Ben Rukovishnikoff-

Alf...are you leaving?

Alf (they shake hands)-

Ben. Yes, for a month or two. What's the deal with the wind, today?

Ben-

If the plane gets here soon it ought to land. The wind is straight up the runway.

Alf-

I need to connect in Anchorage...for a flight to Seattle, then Shanghai.

Ben-

We got out of here in winds a lot worse.

Heidi comes to stand beside Alf.

Heidi-

You'll need a hearse?

Alf-

No! He didn't say that. Ben Rukovishnikoff, this is my...uhh...close friend...Heidi Hoadley. But we didn't know until yesterday.

Ben (shakes her hand)-

Didn't know what?

Alf-

Then they told us to get out.

Ben-

Why? What happened?

(looks at his watch)

I'm due at the museum...a minute ago...to meet Suzi. (looks at Heidi) That's my wife.

Well, Heidi, come to see us when you get back. (he whispers)

Don't sit near the malcontents. Look! There are two more behind them. But...I shouldn't prejudge. Suzi would be mad at me for doing that. The next terrorist you see might be an Aleut.

Alf-

What would the Aleut terrorist do, Ben?

Ben-

He'd yell "Men and children leave! And old ladies. Everyone else drop your pants, and give me twenty bucks...if you have it on you!"

Alf-

I can help you! I'd be handy at that.

Heidi-

Stop it! Don't joke about terrorism. Glad to meet you, Ben.

Lavera (yells)-

Clear the room, please. You all need to reenter, in Order to pass through electronics.

As everyone exits, Alf sees that the loud, heavy man has left a handbag under his seat. A trash can is there, and this would, perhaps, hide the bag.

Because Seven is looking through the glass of the inner windows, Alf gestures with his head in the direction of the bag.

Seven is with two men in red jackets. They enter the cleared area and are stopped by Lavera.

This is when the heavy Moslem, and his thin friend, try to force reentry, pushing others aside.

The men in red jackets apprehend them. Seven gets the bag but doesn't open it; and then he departs with his men and the prisoners.

Act 1 Scene 6

Alf-

The jet has turned north...to go straight out the bay. Goodbye...Mt. Swanson.

Heidi-

Goodbye rainbow. See you again...someday.

Alf-

Maybe in two minutes. There's Mosawi, in the front row. Nah! He sells explosives...he's not a detonator.

Heidi-

He's beside the man with the long beard and the full head of hair. Wait! That's my brown wig.

Alf-

The stewardess is showing how to use seatbelts. Let's watch! She'll feel bad if we don't.

Heidi-

The two other Moslems are at the front...across from Mosawi. Isn't it funny they're always near.

Both the Moslems suddenly jump up, and one puts his arm around the stewardess. He holds a pistol to her head. The other man enters the cockpit.

Mosawi (shouts)-
    Now is not the time! I must get to China!
Heidi-
    The jet is turning again, Alf. Back to town?

Alf jumps up and walks toward the front.

Man with the gun-
    I'll kill her!
Alf-
    Shoot me!
Man with Heidi's wig (stands)-
    Kill me, instead! I'm old...but important.
Man with the gun-
    You die, old man!
    (he shoots, hitting the wig, which sails away)

Alf grabs the man's wrist, and his shirt...then pins him against the cabin wall. Two fishermen, from nearby, secure the man.

Seven (shouts to the stewardess)-
    Get an axe, dear!
Heidi (has drawn her beretta)-
    I'm going in with you!
Alf (beside her)-
    This jet is descending quickly. We couldn't turn to

the runway. He's planning to hit the fuel tanks.

Seven smashes the axe through the door, at the knob, and it flies open; then he goes in...with Heidi following.
(the cabin wall is removed from the stage)
When Alf enters, Seven is trying to revive one of the airline pilots, and Heidi is kneeling over the Moslem man, who is entirely unconscious or dead. Alf gets into the control seat and pulls back on the wheel.

Seven (shouts)-
   Give it gas! No! The other one! Heidi...the one near you...push it!

Alf takes the jet at an upward thrust, in a straight line, over the town and the mountains within and around. Then Seven taps him on the shoulder.

Seven-
   Good job, lad! I'll take it from here. Daughter, you can let up on the gas a bit.
Heidi-
   You can fly it, Dad? How wonderful! Why didn't you do it before?
Seven (gets into the seat)-
   I went halfway through flight school...before my eyes bailed out. Alf...are my glasses on the floor?
Heidi-
   A pilot is awake!
Seven-
   Good for him! And for us, too, I suppose.

Act 2 Scene 1
Shanghai

Alf, Rob, Diane, and Heidi...enter a small park in
Shanghai. There are trees and shrubbery, and mowed
grass. They are not alone in it; a group of elderly
Chinese are gathered.

Alf (to Heidi and Diane)-
   This is the park where deaf people sing. We came
   here last year...after Confucious told me of it.
   (nods his head toward Rob)
Diane (to Rob)-
   What did you see here...that caused you to bring
   my brother?
Rob-
   There was a group of deaf people...exercising...a
   few sitting. And this old man suddenly stood up
   and began singing an Italian opera.
Diane-
   A Chinese man...?
Alf-
   Did you know they were deaf...before he sang?
Rob-
   Yes. Upon arriving I sat near them, Alf...and spoke
   to one and then another.
   (he whispers)
   I think that elderly gentleman was here.

They move a short distance, to a bench beside the
old man. He is apart from a group of six.

Rob (to the old man)-
      I see two little birds in the evergreen tree.
Alf-
      No wonder he doesn't want to hear you.
Rob-
      It's because Chairman Mao tried to have all the
      little birds killed. A few are coming back.

      A man and woman enter, from the south, and are
soon joined by two men, with an old lady close
behind them. All come to the elderly gentleman.
      After greetings, the lady begins to exercise, slowly,
and gracefully. Then the others join in.
      Diane gets up and goes to them, and begins to
exercise. Then Heidi moves to a position nearest to
Diane.
      The Chinese nod and smile.

Alf (to Rob)-
      One thing is certain...you and I won't do that.
Rob (blushes, slightly)-
      Oh, you think not?

      Rob walks to Diane, and begins to exercise. So...Alf
does the same.

Alf-
      I'm not a mindless follower. This bridge seems
      appropriate. I try to step forward from deep inside
      and...doing so...my path is illumined.
Rob-
      A great man said that...I can't think of his name.

The Chinese group stops exercising and bow to each other and the four westerners. Then they sit.

Diane (after returning to the bench)-
   I could live here. I mean...briefly. And I would come to this park every day...it's so relaxing. They take us as part of their life, it seems.
Heidi-
   Briefly? You wouldn't live here...in Shanghai?
Diane-
   I don't like being stared at, even briefly. For instance, on a subway...done without expression... as though they're seeing a lower animal with no feelings of self.
Rob-
   That might be a correct assessment of the way some Chinese see you. That you don't have the intelligence to be offended. But...they sometimes stare at each other.
Alf-
   And so...even though I can be a sight to see...I am allowed to see ignorance in the starer.

The oldest Chinese man suddenly stands and bursts into song. It is an Italian opera.

Heidi-
   He's very good!
Alf-
   Then...he wasn't born deaf.
Rob-
   He is trained, you can tell. What has been long

inside, he knows well.

Diane-

   Now he is alone with what he wanted to be...and wants to be. Without our discrimination, he can get closer to his center...where we all love.

Heidi-

   He's better now?

Diane-

   No! But...it's easier for him to be satisfied. And he could be better, couldn't he?

Rob-

   Surely not in the timbre of his voice. There is a physical necessity which parts of the body rely on. Wouldn't the vocal cord's quality have fallen, along with the power of muscles in the throat and chest?

Alf-

   Perhaps he could have maintained that strength. Though...probably not!

Diane-

   But...as best he can...he can now hear himself being what he wants to be. What would interfere?

Alf-

   Doubt? But...he is with people who love him, and are deaf, too. So he's unconcerned about judgment. And as to respect, doesn't love give sufficiency to a nod and a smile?

Heidi-

   But why is he better?

Diane-

   He has forgotten what he can't do.

Rob-

   No! He no longer cares about what he can't do.

Diane-

   Nothing is between his self...and what his self can
   do.

Rob-

   But...the reality of his physical being stands
   between.

Alf-

   If the two can reach the summit's lip, one part
   short of breath, the unburdened soul can pull up
   the mate. Perhaps. With desire.

Rob-

   To desire it? None of us...even if trained, and deaf,
   would do that. We're happy to only sing in showers.

Alf-

   You think so?
   (his face colors, as he stands and begins to sing)-
   Marie...the dawn is breaking...Marie...my heart is
   aching...to see...blank blank blank blank...blank...
   blank blank...blank blank blank blank...blank...
   blank...Marie...

   Be my love...and with your kisses set me burning;
   one kiss is all I need to know you're mine.
   So...fill my arms the way you fill my dreams, and
   blank blank blank blank blank blaaaank...with
   every sweet desire.
   (he sits)

Diane-

   I didn't know my brother could sing that way.

Rob-

   I did! He didn't come close to what's inside him.

And he couldn't remember the words.

Alf-

He's right! I didn't sing the way I was intending to. I didn't try. To be singing my best might've been to find that my shower voice is pretense, when heard, and I hear it heard. Also, if I sounded great in each set of ears, I would have felt I was showing off.

And...another thing...tough guys don't sing their best.

Heidi-

The heart shows itself fully in some ways and not in others. But you did sing...and I liked it!

Alf-

Kaka! That means "poop!"...where I come from.

Rob-

It's good to remember your roots, Alf. I'm from there.

Alf-

At the park where deaf people sing, I sang.
A pompous ass facing an ancient crowd.
Blind...before the heart of what each wished...
which was...each to each...the love of life.

I...felt lesser statured...and trembled to belong.
I dreamed...shall I throw in a cardboard heart, and
be a head without a dream?
Instead...between thoughts...I promptly sang.

Diane-

Of course...it's always been important to you that all humans are innocent deep inside. So...to feel it in your heart, would make it easier to sing in any way it honestly flows.

You were being heard by us...innocently.

Heidi-

Love rested...as critical minds raced without the
need to. You forgot the words, but I don't care.

Alf-

This is the park where everyman sings to friends.

Rob-

I can agree to that, Alf...but when you sang for us,
was your best necessarily imperfect?

Alf-

Yes. And I sang the way I wanted to.

Rob-

Glad you didn't try to sing like two birds in the
Evergreen tree.

Diane-

We were critical, but we love you.

Heidi-

Also...Alf...I sort of like you.

Act 2 Scene 2

At a Nepali restaurant on Shanghai's XinLe Lu...
New Happiness Street...there are tables to the right
as you enter, but if you walk straight in and a bit to
the left, high-backed wood booths are along the wall.

Alf and Heidi go to a booth adjoining one occupied
by four men, which group includes Mosawi.

The only other animation in this area is an old man
cleaning tables.

As Alf and Heidi sit, Mosawi is at the seat facing
them, and deeper into the building. The two men
whose backs are just there, appear to be Afghanis or
Pakistanis.

Alf realizes, too late, that the benches, which are a
unit with the bench behind it, are at least four inches
lower than he thought. And so...he hits hard against
the booth.

Alf-
    Ow! That hurt! It's way lower than I expected.
Heidi-
    The man behind you is staring. He's quite angry.
Alf (turns his head toward the other booth)-
    Sorry! I misjudged the height.
Heidi-
    I think he wants to hit you.
Alf (in a normal voice)-
    It was an accident. I apologized.
Heidi-
    He's glaring!

Alf (raises his voice)-
   Perhaps the man is a graceless ass!

   Mosawi speaks angrily to the man.

Heidi (waves at Mosawi...then whispers)-
   It's Mosawi. Pretend you like him, Alf.
Alf (looks behind him)-
   Hello. I remember you from Dutch Harbor.

   Mosawi nods.

Alf (to Mosawi)-
   Please tell this man I misjudged the height of the
   seat...and didn't mean to give him a bang.

   Mosawi speaks to the man, then he commences to
ignore Alf and Heidi.
   The old man who is cleaning, takes several articles
from Alf's table, then furtively and deftly places
earphones on their laps. After pointing at a bread
basket at the table's center, he moves away.
   Alf examines the basket, and then plugs his
earphones into it. Heidi does the same.
   Words from the next booth become easy to hear.

Ahmad-
   My name is Ahmad...and, to the glory of us all, we
   have three tasks in Shanghai. First, we attend the
   Chamber Music Concert at Jinan Hotel. Let me
   read from this paper...violin concerto number two
   in D minor, by Wieneawski. Yes, Mr. Barah.

Barah-
　Who...?
Ahmad (continues to read)-
　Soloist Wang Wen. Yes, Mr. Sharan.
Sharan-
　What...?
Ahmad (reads on)-
　And romance in G, by Beethoven.
Barah-
　What is it, again? Who...?
Mosawi-
　To our glory...move on to where we all belong.

　A young man comes from the kitchen. This is Raju.

Raju-
　Can I help you? Good evening, Mr. Mosawi.
Ahmad-
　He is a friend of yours? And he can hear us?
Mosawi-
　I do business with him. Also...I eat here.
Ahmad-
　Bring tea!
　(speaks to the others)
　After Wang Wen, comes the great American
violinist Isaac Sternun...to play Sonata in C minor
by Liszt. Excuse me...in B minor. No!...he plays
something by Mozart.
　Before that we will shoot him!...or blow everyone
there to Hell.
Raju-
　Why?

Ahmad-
   If we die...we shall be taken to Paradise.
Raju-
   I'm from there...and I've had enough of it, as it is.
Ahmad-
   Get tea! You fool!
Mosawi-
   This man is a revolutionary from Nepal...and he
   Is a business partner of mine.
Ahmad (to Raju)-
   Get tea for us!
Raju-
   I will...but if you ever call me fool again, I'll twist
   your nose.

Raju walks away and goes into the kitchen.

Ahmad-
   Also...we will blow up this place.
Mosawi-
   Get on with your speech, please! What happens
   at the hotel?
Ahmad-
   The concert is in three days. Our friend Ahweh
   has all hardware ready, except the explosives van.
   Barah, you will drive the van into the alleyway
   leading to the hotel entrance. Then park it. It will
   only be used if Ahweh fails to kill Mr. Sternun with
   this handgun. You will be near the entrance, to
   observe what takes place within.
Mosawi-
   You will shoot the great violinist before he enters

the music hall?

Ahmad-

Yes...we will stop Mr. Sternun at the doorway of the music room. No one will notice Ahweh in the crowd. He will say "Isaac Sternun...I can play Mozart better than you." When Mr. Sternun stops to look, he will be shot.

Barah-

Then...they will kill young Ahweh...to his glory.

Ahmad-

As this happens, you and Sharan will escape. In five days we must be at the small building which is at the gate of the American Embassy. We will blow it up, and other things.

Barah-

And finally...the tower?

Ahmad-

Seven days from now...the Pearl of the Orient. The explosives will be planted at the tower by Ahweh. But if he's gone to Paradise, Sharan will do it. You and I, Barah, will be on the Huang Pu Ferry. We can have a good view of the collapse.

Barah-

What of the Americans in the next booth? The man has a black shirt, fitting to his neck.

Is he a Christian missionary?

Mosawi-

No! He's a tourist.

Ahmad-

Rich from oil?

Sharan-

I'll stay behind...sit here awhile...then blow them

to Hell, for the glory of God!

Ahmad-

But you must not die here! We need you at the
hotel and the tower. You may stay, if you wish, but
after lighting a couple sticks of dynamite, walk out.

Mosawi-

One stick!...to kill the Americans. You must not
hurt Raju...who will soon buy explosives from me,
in Nepal.

Ahmad-

You only sell them! No commands from you!

Mosawi-

I need to go beyond you, to Nepal. And Raju must
come with me.

Ahmad-

You're a fool! No more talk from you!

Mosawi-

Don't blow yourselves up before you reach the
tower. I won't do that job for you.

Barah-

We will do it! You are not needed!

Mosawi-

You have the two sticks of dynamite. I have a van
load. After you pay me for it, tomorrow...you can
deliver it to the hotel.

Ahmad, Baran, and Mosawi...depart. Sharan stays.

Heidi (whispers to Alf)-

We must act quickly. After the last nitwit leaves.

Alf-

Heidi...sweetheart...empty your purse onto the

table.
Heidi (after she empties it)-
    Don't call me that!
Alf-
    I can cut the fuses with your clippers. Maybe not!
    Look for something to use for pounding.
Heidi-
    A drinking glass.
    (she pours water from one...into a soup bowl)

Sharan now gets up and steps away from his table.
He stops at theirs, and bows.

Sharan-
    Have a happy journey!
Alf-
    Thanks! You, too!
    If joy weeps...we'll be a sight to see, when your
journey ends.

With wide eyes, the man departs.
Once he's gone, Alf leaps to the other table and
finds two sticks of dynamite. The burning fuses are
yet about seven inches long. He puts them onto a
bench and reaches into his pocket for the clippers.
    Heidi comes to him...places the heavy glass near
the dynamite, then steps away.

Heidi (shouts)-
    Clear the area...without delay! It's a bomb!

The old waiter arrives at Alf's side.

Seven-

Good job, Alf! You handled that nicely. Oh!...you already have one cut.

(he takes a tool from his pocket, reaches to the dynamite and cuts the other fuse)

Now you and Heidi get out! Before the police arrive. I should too, I suppose.

Act 2 Scene 3

At the Jing An Hotel, Alf and Heidi, Rob and Diane, sit in the Chamber Music Room. The two girls are between the men, just right of the centered aisle.
   The chamber entrance is on the left, forward.
   One performer has just finished singing.

Rob-
   Sorry I sat so close to the front.
Diane (laughing...in a low tone)-
   How could you know Miss Chen would sing
   Euridice in the style of an elephant? But three
   cheers for the effort. And you have to love her...
   she's smiling so.
Rob-
   And yet...how uncharacteristic of this hotel. Most
   performers I've heard have been sincerely trained,
   and talented. Ask Alf, he was here before.

   They all look at Alf.

Alf-
   She was loud...but maybe they have to perfect
   that first.
Diane-
   But she was several decibels above pleasant.
Heidi (giggling)-
   When that man zipped down the aisle with the
   bouquet of roses, you should have put out your
   foot...Rob...and let him fly. Her screaming hurt my

ears.

Rob-

Can't you forgive the lady?

Alf-

Wait a minute! Have you girls been into the
schnaps? What did you do in the ladies room...that
took so long a time?

Heidi-

You and your old pal with the beard...sometimes
think you know it all...and should always be in
charge. "Go into the ladies room!"..."Open your
purse, and dump it on the table!" Well...Alf...we
know things you don't know. And we'll make you
pay for the times you made us pay. We'll get you in
the end.

Alf-

But there are times when...what you know can
wait awhile. When we shift direction of the herd,
we don't stop to ask your approval. All the horses
would fall.

Diane-

I told her about the difference between the male
and the female. I mean...the way you can see it
show in kids...when a little boy takes something
away from a girl. Usually she will let it happen,
being aware of the difference. But she'll learn how
to teach him, later, about more important things.
Such as...what it is he'll get and not get by being
kind or not kind.

Rob-

Will she love him when he pays the price?

Diane-

    Yes, of course! If she loves him to begin with.

    A girl of eleven or twelve enters through the small door. She has a violin.

Diane (Looks at her program)-

    She's eleven. Beethoven's Romance, in G. I know it well.

Rob-

    Phht! Since when do you listen to classical music?

Diane-

    Since ten years ago...when we divorced, and I got classier. I went from Huxtable to Beethoven.

Rob-

    I see! Well...let's listen to the little bugger.

Heidi-

    The doorway is small. Maybe...so you can't see the performer waiting outside. When is Isaac Sternun coming?

Alf-

    There'll be some fanfare before he enters.

Rob-

    Afterward...if we're alive...want to eat at that Australian restaurant...and have a beer?

Diane-

    It's clear who you asked...since Heidi and I never heard of your Australian restaurant.

Rob-

    We're choosing for you...and knowing you...we know with some certainty whether or not you'd like it.

Diane-
   If you agree to go there...and we don't like it, will
   you admit to a degree of ignorance?
Rob-
   I have a degree in ignorance.
Heidi-
   Diane and I got into the schnaps.

   The little girl begins to play, and she is quite good.
After listening attentively, when the girl finishes,
they join the audience in applauding. Then she
leaves.
   Suddenly...three youngsters, about the age of the
departed violinist, cartwheel in. They traverse the
stage area, then disappear through the same little
door.

Alf (stands)-
   Isaac must be here. I need to go into the hallway.
Diane-
   Be careful, Alf.
Heidi (grabs his sleeve)-
   I'll be at his behind...to protect that part.

   Alf and Heidi go into the hallway which, stage-wise,
is on the other side of a partition.
   In the hall a crowd has appeared, probably mostly
hotel staff and security guards.

Alf (to Heidi)-
   That must be Isaac Sternun...the one without the
   Moustache. Do you see the two older men coming?

Heidi-
     Yes. And Sharan is standing behind us, at the
little door. I'll back up a bit, to be near him.

     One of the older men, with a moustache, waves at
Alf...in a beckoning manner.

Alf-
     Sweetheart! Go to that man...will you?
Heidi-
     Why have my orders changed?
Alf-
     You've been into the schnaps. It's your Dad
beckoning.

     Guards are fighting to clear a path, not only for
Isaac Sternun but for the cartwheeling girls who have
returned, and are heading, again, toward the small
door. Mr. Sternun is smiling, obviously amused.
Now a young man about twenty comes flipping
through. And after two or three turns, he bounds
upward so high that his head is at least ten feet into
the air...at which time he rotates fully. Then he
moves on, in a cartwheeling manner, into the music
chamber.

Isaac (to Heidi)-
     But...can he play Mozart?
Heidi (to Seven)-
     Create a diversion, Dad. Now!
Seven (screams)-
     PiHua! PiHua!

The entire crowd attends to Seven, and this includes two nearby security guards who wrestle him toward the outer door.

Isaac Sternun (to Alf)-
    What did he say? Peewah...?
Alf-
    Dog barking through his other end. I think.
Isaac Sternun-
    Can you see it hit the floor?
Alf-
    Perhaps I should say "Dog speaking through his ass!" But I'm not certain of this.
Isaac Sternun-
    Actually...I'm a violinist. I'll prove it!
    (he smiles...then steps closer to the door)
Alf-
    Let me walk ahead of you, Mr. Sternun.

As the smiling Mr. Sharan, at the door, pulls his hand slowly from his pocket, Alf sees the same small gun given to him by Ahmad at the restaurant. So...he hurries to it, grabs the man's wrist and, raising it high, pins it against the wall.
    The gun fires...then the guard is able to remove it from Sharan's grasp.
    Alf steps to Isaac Sternun and Heidi, who has placed herself between the maestro and the gun. He puts his arm around both.

Isaac Sternun-
    Is the old man all right...at the other end?

Heidi-

He's fine.

Isaac Sternun-

Thanks for your help.

Heidi-

Our pleasure, sir.

Alf-

Thanks for your help.

Isaac Sternun (smiles broadly)-

How did I help?

Alf-

By being able to smile at such times as these.

Heidi-

You're very kind, sir.

Alf-

You live joyously. How can we speak of it?

Isaac Sternun-

Oh! I see! He was barking through his own...other end. The old fart is a hero!

Act 2 Scene 4

Alf, Heidi, Rob and Diane...have crossed the Bund, including the raised area of cement promenading beside the Huang Pu River. They are arrived onto a large ferry which, as they board, is bowing northeast, toward the open sea...about an hour's ride away.

Rob-
   Let's go to the bow, Alf...where we stood last trip.
Alf-
   OK. But I want a look at the stern, first.

They follow Alf to the stern. At its port side...near the dock...they stand facing the Bund and the great buildings of old Shanghai.
   Between the hull and cement of the promenade, the water is covered by drifting lotus plants.

Alf-
   You can see a bit of the Peace Hotel over there. I say that to the ladies.
Heidi-
   To the ignorant among us?
Alf-
   In the water are lotus blossoms. Nice day.
Rob-
   Peaceful...I'd say.
Diane-
   Are we here to watch Mosawi observe an act of terrorism?

Heidi-

Yes...and to see who is with him.

Alf-

He'll be looking across the Huang Pu River to the new city of Pudong...and waiting for the Oriental Pearl Tower to come crashing to the ground.

Heidi-

They'll expect a cavalcade of light.

Rob-

Was that a rock that hit the hull...just under us?

Heidi (her cell phone rings)-

Hi...Dad...yes, we're on the ferry. No...it hasn't left the dock. Everything is fine. How about with you? Good! Just Baran?

(she speaks to Alf and the others)

Limited damage at the embassy. Baran is dead. Dad is now at the Oriental Pearl Tower.

(speaks into the phone)

Dad...? Alf and I leave this afternoon? Get off the boat, you say! Someone has been hired to kill Alf. Oh!...and the Chinese told you to get out. Dad, I can see Mosawi boarding. Goodbye! You be careful!

Rob (leaning over the water)-

Another one hit...right under you, Alf. I think it wasn't a rock...it was a bullet. It was fired from some distance...but let's get away from here!

A loudspeaker announces that the ferry will leave in five minutes.

Alf-

I'll watch the gangplank area, to see who boards.

All four move forward a few yards, until hidden near the entrance to some passenger seating.

Heidi-
   Our plane leaves in four hours, Alf...from the old airport.

A bearded and turbaned, middle aged man, runs across the promenade. He comes slowly up the gangplank, as though to say "You will wait! I am better than you!"...and before reaching the deck, he pulls back a sleeve to study his watch, as though to say "Two minutes early? You will pay for this!"
   After boarding, the man goes forward.

Diane-
   Is he the killer? But...maybe an Irishman is here to do it.
Rob-
   I saw an Irish woman. Anyway...the killer and Mosawi can have a ferry ride.

Alf and the others get off the boat, and stand behind a shoulder-high cement wall which faces the river. They watch the ferry pull away.
   (the lights at the ferry area can be dimmed on stage, this giving the impression of its departure)

Diane-
   Alf...the killer might follow you to Nepal.
Alf-
   If it's one of these...when he walks to me and

smiles, I'll let him think he's got a follower on his hands.

Heidi-

But don't be arrogant, Alf. It's a dark avenue.

Rob-

It's good to be underrated...but keep your eyes open.

Diane-

Tragedy belongs to those who love...but it's a terrible darkness which allows that light.

Rob-

And, Alf...this killer is comfortable in the dark.

Alf-

Why not just say "Goodbye!"? Heidi...what do you think about life? No! Let's go to the airport.

Heidi-

I'm against sexual imposition.

Diane-

A great woman said that. I can't think of her name.

Alf-

Eve...?

Rob-

Animals kill for sex.

Diane-

I know who said that. It was Mr. Dick.

Heidi (puts her hand on Diane's arm)-

No, Diane. It was Mr. Ball's remark.

Rob-

But...animals do kill for sex.

Diane-

What does that have to do with any of us?

Rob-

If I slept with Heidi...Alf wouldn't kill me...he'd kill her. She's the one he dreams of. Also...friendship is important. Of course...he'd kill a Frenchman.

Heidi-

Would you kill me, Alf. Do you care that much?

In the distance, where the Oriental Pearl Tower dimly stands, there is a sharp, small puff of light.

Act 3 Scene 1

In lower Kathmandu...the central square is
addressed as Thamel Chowk. After Alf has walked to
it, he turns his nose left, south, and stops there.

Moneychanger-
Change money? Eighty rupees to the dollar.
Alf-
No, thanks. I already did.
Taxi driver-
Taxi?
Alf-
No, thanks. Maybe later.
Flute seller-
Beautiful music. Only five hundred rupees.
Alf-
No, thanks.

Alf is unaware of Heidi's approach.

Heidi (as she touches his shoulder)-
Alf...! Good morning!
Alf-
Holy...! That surprised me. I must be more alert
when near an edge.

He hugs her...and kisses her on the lips.

Heidi-
What's the meaning of kissing me that way?

Alf-

I love you! At this edge.

Heidi-

I love you, too.

Alf-

That step was quick...and certain.

Heidi-

Alf, we must pledge to be simple, always.

Alf (kisses her)-

Holy...!

Heidi-

Don't say that here, Alf! It shows disrespect.

Alf-

Being silly keeps away the pain. But...from now on I won't say "Holy!". I'll say "Himmel!" That's how the mountain range was named.

Heidi-

How was it named?

Alf-

Many years ago, as a man surveyed, two others looked at the distant heights. One was German, and the other was me...from New Hampshire. Well! The German pointed and said "Himmel!" And I said "Ayeh!

Heidi-

Why are you here? But I'm looking beyond your silliness. A boy delivered this note to me.

(she gives him a piece of paper)

Alf-

I got the same card. "Umesh Shrestha...sandwich room. Sixteen slash one, Thamel Chowk". And on back it says "Look for Mr. Adjikari, Diviner. He'll be on the street".

Heidi-

There's no sandwich shop. I see three hundred people crowding or walking through...and...what?... ten parked taxis, and the smaller ones with the motorcycle wheel. Look!...there's a bicycle cab. Did you ever ride one?

Alf, outside my apartment is dried shit on the stairs. Why did Seven insist I stay there?

But...I like it here.

Alf-

Your square has no toilets or running water...only the one pipe in a central place. You dump your garbage in the street, for someone to take away each morning.

I'm staying at the Potala Guest House...Heidi. The sandwich shop is up this flight of stairs. (points to his right...then speaks to a boy)- Namaste! Do you know Mr. Adjikari?

The boy nods toward a man sitting on a wood stool, at a low table which holds a bundle of sticks and some coins. Other tables are along this side of the street, to the right hand, running south, but those are fruit sellers.

Boy-

He is new here...just today. He is very old, or they would not have let him in.

After thanking the boy, Alf and Heidi walk to the old man.

Heidi (whispers to Alf)-

    He's not old. Maybe early fifties. I can tell by the quality of his voice.

Mr. Adjikari (to a departing figure)-

    Nice to talk with you. Good fortune!

Alf-

    Excuse me, sir! Are you Mr. Adjikari?

Adjikari-

    Good morning, Alf, and Heidi. There are two chairs here. Put them in front of me, please. I want to talk with you.

Heidi-

    Holy...! Dad, do you always need to scare the crap out of us?

Alf-

    You do seem to enjoy it, Mr. Seven.

Seven removes his hat, which is the visorless, soft one, made of cotton, and worn by most Nepali men.

Alf-

    Your hair is all white...and that's not a wig!

Seven-

    I'm Harry Clock...age seventy five. And I often use brown shoe polish in my hair. Sit! Please!

    (they sit)

    Where do we come from? Where do we go? Why are we here? I'd like to know.

Alf-

    At the center of us is the stuff of the universe. Its existence...and ours...has been determined by Consciousness going forward. As love...it maintains itself, and so do we most of the time.

Heidi-

Humans employ little intelligence, but the great
nature of our centers can't be denied.

Seven-

Not by the truth, or by those seeking the truth...
but it can be denied. I think you're right about the
stuff; the driving nature of all things is harmonic
even in chaos...down to the tiniest bit.

Alf-

The tiniest bit. Sure! Where it came from and why
it continues...assures that we are all the same...all
equal.

Heidi-

At our centers. But...most are far from that place.

Seven-

There's the rub. You hate bad action, but you want
to love the center....the innocence...of the person
who performed the act. Can you have that depth of
compassion? Can you be truly "just"?

Alf-

I think I can be "just", to the distance my love can
travel in each case. Is my center hidden from me
or not?

Seven-

We must work hard, sometimes, to see innocence
in the person who hurts another in a way most men
would consider cruel...or self-serving to the point
of madness.

(looks at his watch)

Our job in Nepal is to observe, in order to return
home with proper advice. What do I know? What

have I pondered? If we became revolutionaries in our country, which we have a constitutional right and moral right to do, if we are sincere as to the truth...that is, if the oppression is real...then we would soon be brutal. It is understood by the oppressed that the oppressor is brutal, and so it becomes necessary to match the brutality to be rid of it.

Alf-

The masses in Nepal have been oppressed for centuries. They don't own land; schooling is often unavailable to the poor and low; roads and power sources are few. Government jobs, and voting are privileges owned by the high-caste.

Money entering the country is sucked into the pockets of the King and corrupt officials. This is a Hindu system's high-caste grip.

Heidi-

Being high-caste...they don't consider themselves corrupt, but superior.

Seven-

After long usage of that consideration, the high-caste were schooled...and had exclusive access to Civil Service. Thus...the privileged count and keep incoming money. The low-caste are busy surviving.

Heidi-

And yet...just yesterday some Maoists entered a village, and when a young man refused to join the group, they cut off his hands.

Alf-

Yesterday, the Nepali Army...correction, the

King's Army...entered a village in which three
Maoists were hiding, and killed fifteen villagers.
They laid the bodies on the ground, photographed
them, and had it reported in Nepalnews dot com
that here is a group of Maoists shot dead. And the
world took note of it.

Heidi-

Our country has given money and weapons to
Nepal's government, to aid them against terrorism.
What is the truth of that identification?

Alf-

Do you acknowledge the corruption? Heidi...the
weapons and most of the money went to the king.
Some money journeyed into and around the usual
pockets.

Seven (looks at his watch)-

I'm pleased by your debate. But now I'll speak.
You can't have effective democracy without
separation of church and state. In Nepal the most
high-caste Hindu controls the army, and not long
ago he dissolved parliament, without constitutional
authority. This is the king.

If the rebels succeed in getting power shifted to
the parliament, they will have traveled far. If that
happens, they should pause...perhaps...and let the
world take note of it.

Alf (to Heidi)-

Because the masses believe in reincarnation, they
feel obliged to support caste. Even most poor and
powerless, think God decrees their place in life.

Heidi-

Thinking they get what they deserve...according

to their behavior in the last passage through life.
I'm not entirely ignorant.

Alf (to Seven)-

You think the changes ought to be taken slowly?
At this time, Mr. Seven, you favor giving aid to the
government...to keep the Maoists from going too
far, and losing the sympathy of the people.

Seven-

Yes, Alf...some aid. And the rebels shouldn't kill
the king. Another danger goes beyond loss of
sympathy. Brutality can engulf the innocent in a
"brainwash" sort of way, making them feel they
should support it.

Heidi-

The excess might not offend...it might, instead,
make brutality seem to be necessary?

Seven-

It's best, now, for the rebels to sit at a table and
take a few gains.

Heidi-

We've given M-16s to the government...and have
more coming. Excuse me, Dad...but, yes, I would
advise them to sit, while they yet have asses that
haven't been shot off!

Dad...most institutional religions have got to be
put aside or altered. They're a large part of man's
misery through the ages. Do you agree?

Seven-

Yes! But remember...most who seek Divinity can't
do it from within their own ethics. You can...they
can't. Be kind to their weakness.

(looks at his watch)

The man with the turban, the killer, will be here in a couple minutes. If he sees you leaving my table, he'll ask about you. I'll tell him you'll be on the bus to Pokhara...this evening, at eight.

Heidi-

Do you have a working relationship with the police?

Seven-

The commissioner said I pay him two thousand rupees a day, or leave the country by Wednesday.

Heidi-

And so...?

Seven-

I've got four days. Listen! I have another man with me, and he'll be on the bus to Pokhara. Ergo...more brutality!

Go to the palace, Alf, and show Heidi the high walls topped with sharp iron spikes. And show her the front gate. There'll be action there soon.

Then go to the zoo, because Mosawi and Raju will be there at five...to meet a revolutionary. Be there at four thirty, on a park bench...kissing.

At eight...be at the Greenleaves Restaurant. Be disguised. The tables are outside, in a courtyard. I'll lead you to one. Order tea and dinner, and I'll give you earphones. Mosawi and Raju, and others, will be at the next table.

Here comes the turbaned man. Get going! And don't look back!

Act 3 Scene 2

At the Kathmandu Zoo all cages are cruel...in the dominance of steel bars and cement. Alf and Heidi have arrived at one about six feet square, in which there are two dead porcupines. In the cage's food bowl is a large rat, eating.

Alf-
　　Excuse me, sir! Do you have a key to this cage?

The man shuffles to them, leans against the cage, and looks inward.

Man-
　　No, I don't! Sorry! Explosives have come through Kashmir and very northeast India. Our friends have one van load.
Heidi-
　　Dad! I swear to God! Next time whistle "Dixie" before you suddenly appear.
Seven-
　　Our friends have established contact with two Nepalis. One of them ought to be here soon. So... Mosawi will have the van load, and this Nepali will drive it away. Tonight, at Green Leaves Restaurant, Raju will pay for it in the company of the contacts. and because I'll lead you to a table beside theirs, you must disguise yourselves.
　　When I need to appear to you...unannounced... I'll sing "Unforgettable", like Nat King Cole.

Heidi (to Alf)-
    Shall we sit by this cage?

    Seven gives Alf a black, leather bag of the size, in inches, of a ten by ten egg carton.

Seven-
    Yes, sit here. I've bugged every bench. I can
    activate the one they're at...by pressing a button.
Alf-
    There's Mosawi and Raju.
Seven-
    They'll sit near the gate. So...I, too, will be there.
    (he shuffles away)
Alf-
    Heidi, remember when Seven was Mr. Adjikari, at
    his table in Thamel? Which is he...Adjikari, the
    noble and wise...or this one? Look! He's carrying
    the hammer, high...and shuffling toward those men
    as though to say "I'll knock you on the head!"
Heidi-
    Alf, I think he acts as an idiot...to be underrated.
Alf-
    Another man has come through the gate, and is
    approaching the others.
Heidi-
    And yet...they only attend to Seven. They're ready
    for him! Raju has his fat briefcase held as a shield.
    Alf, you better help the old fart.

    Seven has stopped at a cage about twenty feet
from the men. With the hammer...he pounds a staple

onto the fencing at a corner post. Then he bends
over, as though to retrieve something he dropped.

Seven-
    Can you hear anything?
Alf (into his microphone)-
    Yes, Mr. Clock...pounding hearts.
Heidi-
    Dad...you scared them. They're ready to fight. No!
    Wait...! They're settling down...and speaking to the
    man who just arrived. Be careful!

    Raju stands, and greets the newcomer. Mosawi
remains seated, and when the man extends his hand
to him, he doesn't take it.

Raju (to the newcomer)-
    I'm Raju. My father's name was Sanu, and he
    joined the trekking company you work for. When I
    was little I visited your office. I met Bhim, Damm...
    and Besudhev.
Mr. Kuerile-
    Also you met me, many toimes. My name is Mr.
    Kuerile. I knew your father...and I remember you.
Raju-
    This is Mr. Mosawi. He loves money more than
    man. He would blow off your head if I gave him
    seven hundred rupees.
Mosawi (waving both arms near his own face)-
    You have no right to malign me! I sell explosives,
    and you buy them!
    (speaks to Mr. Kuerile)

I have a van load...which has arrived from the China border.
Mr. Kuerile-
    From Tibet? Do you mean from the far western part?
Mosawi-
    Can you agree to buy it, if I show it to you?
Raju-
    I'm the buyer! Remember that!
    Mr. Kuerile, if you and your group agree to take the explosives, I'll buy them.
Mr. Kuerile-
    Tonight, at the Green Leaves Restaurant, my boss will decide that. I'll look at it, and recommend it to him. Can I take the van?
Raju-
    Yes, take it!
Mosawi-
    No! Before it has been bought...it belongs to me. You can look at it now...and then tonight you can tell us whether or not you accept it.
Raju-
    Take it!
    (hands the keys to Mr. Kuerile)
    I trust you to bring it back as it is. The red van... just there, outside the gate.
Mosawi (snorts, and looks away...then recovers)-
    I'll show you how to strap explosives to your back and walk undetected into a crowded restaurant...or onto a bus. Yesterday I passed a movie house, and saw hundreds milling about. Better yet...to the lap of the king. I'll show you how!

Mr. Kuerile-
   You'll show us nothing!
Raju-
   When this deal is finished...perhaps we can show
   Mr. Mosawi the way to the border.

   Seven begins to shuffle toward the three men.

Seven-
   Que hora es? What is the time? Por favor!
   (he raises the hammer)
   I need to repair you!

   The men move from the bench and, as Seven
begins to pound a nail into it, they go through the
gate into the street. Then the van and taxi depart as
Alf and Heidi arrive.

Heidi-
   Dad, why did you speak Spanish? They don't use
   that language here.
Seven-
   I'll see you both at Greenleaves.

   Seven removes a device from the underside of the
bench, and then shuffles away, into the park. It
seems evident he will visit other benches.

Alf (sits on the bench)-
   Heidi...sit here a minute. I need to tell you a story.
   The man who departed in the van...Mr. Kuerile...is
   an acquaintance of mine, from a six day trek, taken

four years ago.

When I leave Kathmandu, I often travel by bus to Jiri, then walk east about five days to Lukla, where you turn north to Everest. Well...it takes me three days to get used to walking ten or eleven hours, up and down. I hired Mr. Kuerile to carry half my load to Lukla. And for the entire trek he was bitching. He was cranky.

Heidi-

Because you walked eleven hours a day, up and down? Sorry! Get on with your story.

Alf-

He was fifty seven, then...and said he had six kids.

For helping me he expected to get four or five dollars. Well, after we arrived at Lukla, he got drunk at dinner, so I decided to pay him in the morning. I went to my room. Then he banged on the door...and asked if I planned to not pay him.

Heidi-

He figured you were angry about his having a drink...and for having been cranky.

Alf-

Sure!

But, Heidi, I knew Mr. Kuerile had been jazzed around many times. I figured that was why he got cranky from the first steps we took. Now...I paid him more than he expected, including money for dinner the next day or two in case he missed the Kathmandu plane. And I gave him a decent tip. All of which...to you and me...was not much, maybe thirty or forty bucks. But to him it could have been a third of a year's income.

When I awoke in the morning, I was surprised that
he was asleep on the other bunk. Also...I was
dismayed, because the night had been a freezing
one and he had no blanket or jacket. He wouldn't
ask the higher caste hotel people for a blanket.

I threw my parka over him.

That morning we got to talking...this fifty seven
year old and I. Did I tell you he has six kids? He
said "What do you think of communism? I might
vote communist, next toime."

Heidi-

Oh, my God! Alf...what did you tell him?

Alf-

That with a majority communist government, he'd
revel briefly...thinking he was free of caste, and
hoping to own land. But neither one would happen.
What he would have is capitalism for rich Hindus
with the words "communist majority" tacked on.

He'd have empty words.

I had a deep breath, as I sat across from this man
who makes a hundred dollars a year, maybe. Mr.
Kuerile...who spends his life on dirt, usually not far
from the clean, black tar surrounding the palace
and the streets running from it, where sit the shops
of the privileged.

Yes, the king...called the fourth richest man in the
world.

Then I said to Mr. Kuerile..."You need change. If I
were you...I'd vote communist."

Heidi-

You wanted to help him open a door? But...now
you seem sorry that you did.

Alf-

   He has no vote. Not then, and not now. There is no
Constituent assembly in Nepal. Only the high caste
have that privilege.

Heidi-

   For Mr. Kuerile...what to do, Alf?

Alf-

   Heidi...all Nepal knows that millions of dollars
enter as airport taxes, visas, trekking permits,
climbing fees. Also...foreign aid. And almost none
of it benefits the people.

   What to do? Smash the bastards...so they can't
control voting. Make them pay for the centuries of
shit...the people have been told to love.

Heidi-

   Told so often, they accepted it for centuries.
But, Alf...isn't this explosive advice? Most of them
remain Hindus. They want to be finished with the
mud...but not offend God's decrees.

Alf-

   Yes! They're ready to kill, but need to feel they
have the right...through God...to do so.

   Here comes Seven.

   Seven walks briskly to them. He has a packsack
and a leather handbag. Once arrived, he smiles.

Seven-

   And yet...you look so glum. Lovers ought to laugh.

Heidi-

   Dad...we're not lovers. Yesterday, for a moment,
we felt some attraction to one another. I've almost

forgotten it. Do you remember it, Alf?

Alf-

It seems ages ago. "I sort of like you"...is all right.
Let's try that!

Seven (laughs)-

Bullshit! Why are you stepping in it? Ahh! Give me
a smile. Even the tragic is allowed by love.

Do you think I didn't see you in Thamel, kissing?

Heidi-

Dad...will you arrest Mosawi?

Seven-

Tonight, perhaps.

Heidi-

Will you arrest those he sells explosives to?

Seven-

If they seem unnecessarily brutal...or have power
and money firing their dreams.

Most of all...the revolutionary loves the light in the
darkness. He loves equality.

Alf-

How can you tell who is a revolutionary...and who
is pretending to be.

Heidi-

Remember...I heard that Moaists entered a village
and, upon refusal of a young man to join them, cut
off his hands. If that report is true, who did the
cutting...the one who loves the light in the dark, or
the one who wants to rob?

Alf-

I think any man can arrive at brutality, but some
will deepen it...and degrade humanity. I would kill
a man who is monumentally unjust...but, hopefully,

it's only his act I hate, after the dust settles.
Seven-

    The man who loves the light in the darkness, sees it in all men...there at the center of each. The true revolutionary, even as he kills, holds all others to be the same as himself.

    The thief is separate...the hands he cuts off are not in any way his own.

Alf-

    Do we allow for confusion and desperation...when what is loved seems to be at the point of death? How do you judge brutality then...in those who have lost control of judgment, and know they've lost it. But...in not knowing what to do, they continue to do that which might be correct, because it seems doing nothing only serves death.

Seven-

    Confusion needs to be ended...even if its cause elicits compassion. If the action is wrong, in our judgment, we stop it or try to.

    Tonight, at the restaurant, we can listen for expectations and desires. And, we must be aware that for rebellion in Nepal, a place of desperation seems to be at hand.

Heidi-

    And so...chaos could enter?

Seven-

    Five thousand M-16 rifles have arrived. Given by the United States to the Nepali Army...correction, the King's Army. And weapons are coming from Belgium, including five hundred sub-machine guns. Also...the king has turned an Indian Army General into a Nepali one...thinking to put that possibility onto the neck of the revolutionary.

Alf-

Mr. Seven...the man who was standing at this bench portered for me, four years ago. Mr. Kuerile. I advised him to vote communist...thinking that, for him, change is a good prospect by almost any name.

Did I help him get ready to die?

Act 3 Scene 3

At the edge of the street, head-high fencing, of
latticed wood strips, fronts Greenleave's courtyard.
Alf and Heidi pass through its swinging, metal-spear
gateway.
   (half the fence is pulled from the stage)
   The courtyard has a dozen umbrella-covered tables.
Beyond...directly inward, is the restaurant's hotel. To
the right, four Nepalis are making music.
   Heidi is wearing a white blouse under a grey vest. A
red bandana hides her hair, and a black mask covers
her eyes.
   Alf has a white shirt with a black vest, and a Nepali
hat of visorless, thin cotton. He has a fake, longish
nose, and a moustache.
   A waiter comes to them. He is wearing a white
vest, a white wig, and very thick glasses. Walking
fully upright...rather stiffly...he leads them to a part of
the courtyard farthest from the front, to the northeast
corner, quite near the hotel wall.

Waiter (suddenly sings)-
   Unforgettable...that's what you are.
   Unforgettable...though near or far.
   (he smiles, and speaks in a normal tone)
   Sorry to be so distant from the gate, but this is
   away from the music stand. And the lighting is
   lower...but romantic.
Alf-
   I'd say it's unforgettable, too.

Heidi-
    You scared the hell out of me, anyway...Dad.

    At a white-cloth covered table under an umbrella,
Seven seats Heidi to face the center, and puts Alf on
her left, to face the street fence.
    He gives them menus and places a receiver beside
a bowl with flowers overhanging.

Seven (nods toward the table Alf faces)-
    I'll try to seat them there...but this place will soon
be full.
Heidi-
    Even as we think of them, they enter.
    (puts her hand on the old man's shoulder)
    Remember not to shuffle, Dad. They'd recognize
you as the lunatic from the zoo.
Alf (as Seven moves away)-
    You persist in calling him Dad. That's sweet.
Heidi-
    In my heart he is. Or...I never had one to know. I
often thought that if my real Dad had lived he would
have been like Seven.
Alf-
    It's a nice compliment...to both.
    But, Heidi...why is he wearing that loop of cord at
his belt?

    At the next table, Seven seats Mr. Kuerile, Mosawi,
Raju, and a stranger...who is a heavy-set, middle age
man.
    Seven places the stranger farthest from Alf. The

others sit where they please, which is Raju facing
away from the center of the restaurant, and Mr.
Kuerile toward it, as does Heidi. Mosawi's back is
there for Alf to see.

When Seven puts menus onto the table, the
stranger doesn't take one but, instead, looks at his
watch.

Stranger (Mr. Narayan Dahal)-
   Only tea. I must leave soon.

The others order. This is done by Raju and Mr.
Kuerile in Nepali. Then Seven nods, and departs.

Mr. Dahal-
   Mr. Mosawi...I have been told the shipment is
   satisfactory. What amount do you wish to be paid?
Mr. Kuerile-
   Oh, no! Mr. Raju Lamichane will buy it.
   (nods his head toward Raju)
Mr. Dahal (checks his watch)-
   I control it!
   We need to use it...in the vehicle. As day arrives,
   the king will come...supposedly...from the palace
   gate and turn east, for his way to the airport.
Alf (whispers to Heidi)-
   The King will turn to his left.
Mr. Dahal-
   At the end of the palace block is an alleyway from
   which he will come...as the escort turns south.
Alf (whispers)-
   As the King's escort turns to their right.

Raju-

Why not blow up the gate, tonight, and hurt no one? This will say to the people that the King's rule must end. Killing the King will rouse the people against us. And...that act is more brutal than I want to be.

Mr. Dahal-

It's no longer effective to strike to the edge of things. Blowing up a gate...will end a gate's rule.

Mr. Kuerile (both hands against his forehead)-

I am ready to kill. But...there are rumors about peace talks.

Mr. Dahal-

A stalemate...even if it led to elections in which we gained a slight majority...would find the same corrupt leaders yet in Parliament. We need total victory.

It is decided by the world...especially by Mr. Bush, that we are terrorists. So...let's fulfill the brutal part of that, and avoid a stalemate.

Mr. Kuerile-

Some already have been to excess.

Mr. Dahal-

A few. But the government calls us all terrorists. The support of the people is fading within the lies and the truth. Now, only increased brutality can win the war for us. We need major victories. We are the People's Army, but the King's Army is being given weapons and money from beyond Nepal.

Mosawi (leans toward the stranger)-

Destroy big things...the King, his palace, buildings of Parliament...the Army! Listen! Explosives put in

a garbage can, near the alley, and detonated even
as the King is arrived, will turn him back. By that
time your truck is behind him. The King will die!
Raju-
   This is bloodthirsty. Such murder is not needed.
The Nepali people would hate us for such brutality.
Mr. Dahal (raises his voice)-
   You are new at this! Try doing it six years! Then
tell me not to kill the King!
Mr. Kuerile-
   And yet...it is not for me. The explosives must be
used to make anxiety in the government...so they
will agree, soon, to many of the Maoist demands.
Some day I will own land...and my children will.
Raju-
   The control of the Nepali Army will be transferred
to a democratic government. Political leaders will
no longer be corrupt...once they have the power to
be rid of one another through voting.
Mr. Dahal-
   You dream! Without massive killing, the Hindu
system will go on. Caste...which can't be legislated
away...will go on. The King will wear velvet. Your
children will walk barefoot on dirt, near the palace.
Raju-
   With excess...we can lose an election, if it comes.
There are two things you failed to mention. If
corruption passes from the government...and the
Nepali Army is transferred to that government...
other progress will follow from that.
Mr. Dahal (shouts)-
   Such dreams!...as aid comes from Mr. Bush, and

others, to help the King and the corrupt leadership stay as it is.

Mosawi-

Kill the oppressors with more intensity! You must go to big targets!

Mr. Dahal-

Yes...they will be cut to their knees.

Mr. Kuerile-

They will be brought to the tables.

Mosawi (to Dahal)-

I'll take you to the vehicle.

Raju-

A good democracy has separation of church and state, a condition beyond legislation. But, if war ends now, peacefully, many changes will occur. In the government, those who wish to serve all...have taken note of our words.

Mr. Kuerile-

I have been poor all my life...and if my children and grandchildren face the same...this sharpens my sight to kill. Yet I think Mr. Raju Lamichane is correct. There will be changes made at the table.

Mr. Dahal-

How long will it be, Mr. Kuerile? How many years have I fought? Six! How many years before you kill?

Mr. Kuerile-

Seven!

Mr. Dahal-

The world is handing machine guns and M-16s to The King's Army.

Mr. Kuerile (again holds his head)-

Am I in a dream?

Raju-
    There will be changes.
Mr. Kuerile-
    Oh...to be a head without a dream.
Alf (again whispers to Heidi)-
    Resting on a cardboard heart.

Seven returns carrying a tray holding bottled beer.

Seven (leans toward them and whispers)-
    Follow Mr. Kuerile and Raju. See where the
    explosives go...then call me.
Alf-
    What is that cord on your belt? Now I see that it's
    attached with a carabiner. What's at the other end?
Seven-
    Handcuffs.

Seven begins to move away as though intending to
pass the next table but, when almost to it...he falls. A
quart-size unopened bottle of beer goes under Raju's
table. Seven follows it.

Heidi-
    What is he up to, Alf?
Alf-
    Let's go, sweetheart.
Heidi-
    Does that give meaning to your kiss...and your
    remark about loving someone?
Alf-
    Yes...now let's go! We've got to be outside when

Raju and Mr. Kuerile exit...in order to follow them without suspicion.

After walking quickly to the gate, they look back and see all four men leap to their feet. After Mosawi falls back into his chair...as though pulled downward from below...the others proceed to depart, as two Nepali policemen come from the hotel toward the table.

Alf and Heidi exit.

Act 3 Scene 4

On a two-engine plane, sturdy and boxlike, the sole
pilot has loaded his craft in such a way that Alf is
beside him, and Heidi is at Alf's back. The seat to her
left, and the next five rows...also the aisle...are filled
with baggage. Behind the baggage sit two Nepali
men.

Alf (to the pilot)-
   I remember you from years ago. The plane was
similar, but we had a dozen passengers, on a flight
from Kathmandu to Lukla.
Pilot-
   I fly that way now, but not often. There are fewer
trekkers and climbers. Some persist...mainly for
Everest and Ama Dablam.
   You might be confronted on the trail and asked to
pay a fee...of perhaps ninety dollars. Then they'll
smile and give a receipt.
Alf-
   Maoists...or opportunists?
Pilot (smiles)-
   Just yesterday I carried dynamite to Jiri, for two
men who said they would build bridges over the
Kolo and Soto rivers.
   One spoke of going home to Phermionboche. You
go two hours from Jiri, on the Everest trail...then
come back in a northwest manner an hour or so.
Alf-
   I've seen it on a map. It's just northeast of Jiri.

Pilot-

You go to Yarsa, and step behind an outhouse. There is a trail no outsider knows about...except some of us. Then you pass through a cave, but it's only twenty feet through it. After leaving it...soon enough you go straight up to Phermionboche. You can see Jiri again...below you...in the direction of Kathmandu.

Heidi-

Phermionboche. Is it like Shangrila?

Pilot (continues to speak to Alf)-

They grow millet and a few potatos. Not much. Some chickens. But...just over the hill, above town, is an apple orchard.

Mr. Kuerile...I think he wants to fill his house with dynamite.

(he laughs)

If someone stumbles into town, Maoist or Nepali Army, and makes trouble, he can blow them away.

Do you blame him? You're an American. Who should he kill?

Alf-

Not anyone...but, if someone...then a terrorist of any name.

Pilot-

I don't blame the poor for fighting. But...the Hindu System and the King will prevail.

Today, I carry M-16 rifles for the Nepali Army. These are made in America. Also...there is a box from Belgium.

Alf-

Submachine guns, probably. Are these all for Jiri?

Pilot-

Only a dozen troops are there. Some of these guns will go east to posts on the Everest trail...and to Lukla. That's where you turn north to Everest...as you know. I said that for your wife...if she listens. Will you walk that far?

Alf-

No! We'll try to avoid the ninety dollar robbery.

Pilot-

Such greed hurts our country. So...you look ahead. You have a beautiful wife...I say with respect, and not trickery. I, too, have a beautiful wife.

Heidi-

Do you say it to her, sometimes?

Again the pilot ignores her.

Alf-

One time when I rode the bus the eleven hour ride from Jiri to Kathmandu, the men sat...and the women and kids stood in the aisles, all the way. That's what she meant.

Pilot (shrugs his shoulders)-

My wife has been putting me in my place.

Heidi-

Beside her?

The pilot doesn't answer.

Heidi-

When you are beside her...are you lower than before? I'm not trying to be rude...I'd like to know

if you think you and your wife are equal in any way.
Pilot (looks at her)-

In a Hindu society it is often true that when a man
kills his wife...the authorities will say she deserved
it. I can put my wife out. But I do love her...and she
has given me a son.
Heidi (after a moment)-

No daughter?
Pilot-

Yes, a daughter, too.
Heidi-

I don't know what is fully in your heart. To be fair,
I think that you, also, don't know.

On this ride one sees much that is beautiful. Do
you take it for granted? Do you think about it? We
all take things for granted, sometimes.
Pilot-

This is my home.

(he sighs)

I thought my father and mother would be here
forever, in the sense that I didn't think about their
deaths...until they died. Yes...I could attend more
to the things I love. But, I do know what are the
proper levels of concern for me. I am a high-caste
Hindu.
Heidi-

I see that the two low-caste Hindus are sitting in
the back...behind the baggage. This is one of the
concerns you attend to. Do you think it's proper
that I should be quiet?
Pilot (after a few minutes)-

And yet...I'm not angry at you.

Yesterday I had dynamite...today I have guns. How
do I attend to that?

Now I ask without rudeness...is one of you the
boss, or are you equal?

Heidi-

We are equal. When I defer to my husband, it is by
my choice.

Alf, why are you letting me do all the talking?

Alf-

I thought you wanted to. I spoke of the long bus
ride...during which two kids sat on my knee, at
different times, five or more hours...putting my leg
to sleep.

Pilot-

Is there nothing wrong with your country?

Alf-

Self-service and greed flourish. Unions have driven
wages and prices so high...most goods are made in
other countries. The jury system...a feeding trough
for attorneys...is costly and slow.

Washington's politicians have "pay me" pockets.
And...lobbyists put money into those deep holes.

Heidi-

Few Americans would say it, Alf...about unions
and the jury system. They once served our country
well. Now...although they do injury, we're told
repeatedly we ought to love them. So...they begin
to tear us apart.

Alf-

In our society...as in most others...we're told
things early in life...so often...we can become deaf
and blind to any different conclusion about them.

Pilot-

Among the explosives, there is a small box for a Mr. Whitmore and wife. Do you know them?

Alf-

I'm Alf Whitmore. This is Heidi. And you are...Mr. Bahadur?

Pilot-

Sanu Bahadur.

Alf-

Mr. Bahadur...what of the man who was with Mr. Kuerile? Was it Raju Lamichane, of Jiri?

Pilot-

Yes! He said...before he left Nepal, his playmate was a girl named Indu...who had recently moved to Jiri.

Then...Mr. Kuerile called Indu his daughter.

Alf-

Raju was eight when he left Nepal.

Pilot-

Now Indu has a seven year old child...and has lost her husband.

Heidi-

Also...we must attend to fate.

Pilot-

Mr. Kuerile was pleased Raju's life touched his.

Act 3 Scene 5

After having walked four hours from Jiri, east and then northwest, Alf and Heidi stand atop a steep climb. They face two boulders with a trail between.

Alf-
   This is the doorway to Phermionboche.

   Shouting is heard, in Nepali...some distance ahead.

Heidi-
   Is someone coming, Alf?
Alf (takes a pistol from a shoulder holster, and puts it into his pocket)-
   Hope I don't need to use it.
Heidi-
   What if it's fake Maoists wanting to rob us? Let's hide in the trees...over here, to our left.
Alf-
   Too late!

   Four young western men appear, between the boulders.
   At sight of Alf and Heidi, the man in front holds up his hand, palm forward.

Heidi-
   These are not the men I heard.
First man-
   G'day to ya! Don't go into the village...or you'll be

robbed.

Second man-

The bastards are sitting at the other side of town. if you wait a few minutes they'll be gone.

Third man-

Yeh...they got seven thousand rupees from each of us, the bloody murderers.

The young men appear to have not washed in a few weeks, except for some dousage in streams. Also, they seem tired and in a naturally bad mood.

First man-

We came from Everest Base Camp...by way of Gokyo, and then west from Thame. Know what I'm saying, mate?

Alf-

Yes, I know of it.

Second man-

If I had a gun I would have parted their balls. Shit! Now I'm almost broke.

Alf-

How many are there?

First man-

Eight. All with rifles. Two or three have pistols, as well.

Second man-

When I looked back they were sitting at the far side of the square...having tea...from thermoses.

Alf-

How unlike a Nepali...that they won't stop along the way and spend a few cents for tea, or have a

campfire. They must have stolen the thermoses.
Second man-

That's right, mate! And now they have mine!
Third man-

One spoke of going to a place just below Jiri...to
wait for a bus from Kathmandu, so they can rob it.
Heidi-

What else happened...in Phermionboche? You
called them murderers.
First man-

They killed a young man who refused to pay them.
He was face down in the dirt, when they walked
away to have tea. A girl was crying...and I heard an
older man whisper to a villager that he would soon
blow up those friggers...eight toimes. That's the
way he said it...friggers and toimes.
Alf-

Was the dead man's name Raju?
First man (scratches his head)-

I think so. Raju. Yes...that was it.
Alf-

If they're going to Jiri, why are they sitting to the
northwest of the square and not coming this way?
First man-

If you leave northwest and go down to the river,
you can follow it into town. They say walking is
slow that route...but you could hide more easily.
Heidi-

Do they have uniforms?
First man-

Nah! Some military boots and pants. But their
jackets are like ours and yours.

The young men depart, and are soon out of sight on the sharply descending trail.

Alf and Heidi look ahead.

(the two boulders are removed from the stage)

They see the village square...which centers a water pipe spigot and cistern, and two tables. The cistern is a rock-lined pool, cemented...and is for washing clothes, because it continually overflows into an open-top rock pathway carrying excess water to the southeast corner of town and then away, downward.

Beyond the tables at the northeast side of the square are a pair of windowless, two-story buildings, of rock and wood. The rocks have stucco on them and are painted white. All wood is bare, including that of their porches.

Ten people are at the center of the square, at a table covered by white sheets, and edged by flowers, most of them red. On the sheets is the body of a young man with hands folded across his chest.

As Alf and Heidi approach, two kneeling figures turn their heads, slightly.

Alf (with hat off and head bowed, he whispers)-
    It's Mr. Kuerile and Indu...kneeling.
Heidi-
    It is Raju who died. Oh, my God! How awful!

They walk to about eight feet away, then again bow their heads...standing respectfully still.

Mr. Kuerile (stands and faces them)-
    A son of the village has died. No! I should say it

right...and many toimes. He was murdered...by thieves calling themselves revolutionaries. Do I know you?

Alf-

Mr. Kuerile...my name is Alf Whitmore. We once walked together, from Jiri to Lukla. And my wife and I met Raju in Shanghai. We are saddened and angry that he is killed. How hard it must be for you.

Mr. Kuerile-

Soon we will take his body northwest of here, down to the river...where two meet. The Kolo and the Soto. Then...after the Puja...his ashes will be put into the river, and some onto land.

You are welcome here.

(points to a small, windowed house at the east side)

My wife will fix food for you. And you can stay. But you should not be here tomorrow, because the men who killed Raju might come back.

I will fight them.

Alf-

I will stay to help you.

Mr. Kuerile-

I have explosives...and will put some between the boulders and where the trail comes up from the river at the northwest corner. And I will put some here...at the center.

Alf-

Do you have detonators and wire...and batteries?

Mr. Kuerile (steps to Alf)-

Now I remember you. In Lukla I asked you about communism. You told me you hate it, then you said

I need change in my life...so maybe I should vote
for it.
Alf-
　Are you sorry for the fighting?
Mr. Kuerile-
　No! Our country has the privileged...and the shit.
It has a King, self-satisfied politicians, fat business
men...and low-caste dirt-sweeps. So, here am I,
with my daughter and my wife. In Kathmandu are
five more of my children...and guess what they are,
many toimes.
Alf-
　Also...your country has the men who killed Raju.
And they do whatever else that pleases them.
Mr. Kuerile-
　They rob from anyone. Much food has been taken
from us,
　By calling themselves Maoists, our revolution is
hurt. I must go now. I will be many hours at the
ceremony.

An old holy man now walks from between the
boulders, and comes to the square. He is wanting to
put Tika upon those present, but the mark is already
on the forehead of most.

Alf (to Heidi)-
　Maybe this Brahmin will go to the river and help
perform the ceremony.

The old man comes to them and puts a red mark on
their foreheads, then goes to the body and kneels.

Alf –

    Is it possible this old man is someone we know!

    Alf goes to the old man and kneels beside him, briefly. Then he returns to Heidi.

Heidi-

    What did he say, Alf?

Alf-

    He said nothing. He's crying.

Act 3 Scene 6

On the porch of Mr. Kuerile's building, Alf and Heidi
are standing near the doorway, and Seven is at a
table beside them.

Alf-
    The square is entirely empty, and yet I assume Mr.
    Kuerile left someone to watch the village.
Seven-
    Maybe the three of us.
Heidi-
    Why don't you change into regular clothing, Dad?
    Someone will find you out.
Seven-
    And yet I am religious. To me...God is the focal
    point of universal awareness. He is the Ground of
    Being...at the center of things, including each of us.
    So...even though I hate bad action, I try to feel the
    nature of that center.
    I hate the "I am better than you" part of humanity,
    which I condemn as weakness...and ignorance.
    I believe fate brings us to the bridges, but we can
    choose to cross or not. We each have a best path,
    and ought to follow it.
Alf-
    Look! Mr. Dahal and four other men have come
    from behind the boulders.
Seven-
    Here is the man M-16s have beaten into a blind
    brutality. Let's have a picnic.

Heidi-

 Dad, your bitterness is showing.

Seven-

 Dahal is wanting the explosives to kill the King, but we'll hope a busload of children doesn't get in the way. There he is...thinking the end justifies any means. Alf...go kill all of them!

Heidi-

 Dad! Would you give that order?

Seven (sighs deeply)-

 All three of us will go out...to keep them from getting the explosives.

Heidi-

 I'm surprised you want us to interfere directly in someone elses war.

Seven-

 Think of the busload of children.

Alf-

 We'll defend little ones...and Mr. Kuerile's place.

Seven-

 Dahal would consider the explosives to be public property. But I feel as you do.

Heidi-

 An old man and woman are walking to the water spout.

Mr. Dahal (shouts)-

 Where is Mr. Kuerile? And why is the village quiet?

Old Nepali man (calmly)-

 A band of robbers came...and killed young Raju Lamichane. All villagers went to the Kriya.

 (points to the northwest)

 Down where the rivers fork.

Mr. Dahal-
>And how long will he be gone?

Old Nepali man-
>Two more hours...perhaps. It is not yet noon.

Old Nepali lady (louder than her husband)-
>Why do you ask?

Mr. Dahal-
>That's my business!

Old Nepali lady-
>Do you come to rob?

Mr. Dahal-
>I come to get what belongs to me.

Old Nepali man-
>Mr. Kuerile will come. We'll bring tea. Sit!

Mr. Dahal (looks at his watch)-
>We must go. Robbers took our money...last night,
>on the bus. We have a ride to Kathmandu, at three.
>take us to where Mr. Kuerile put the explosives.

Old Nepali lady-
>You can wait for him!

Mr. Dahal-
>Take us to it...or we'll search your houses.

Old Nepali lady-
>Search! You will find nothing.

Mr. Dahal-
>Then...we'll burn your houses to the ground.

Alf (to Seven)-
>I'm going out there.

Seven-
>We all will, Alf.

As they step from the porch, Alf goes ahead. Dahal

immediately faces them.

Mr. Dahal (speaks mainly to Alf)-
 If you get in the way, I'll kill you! We have pistols.

 After saying this, Dahal seems to dismiss Alf as a
threat. Again he speaks to the old Nepali lady.

Mr. Dahal-
 The building behind you...if I find nothing there, I'll
burn it to the ground.

 Alf goes to Dahal, grabs him by the shirt, at the
neck and, in a twisting motion, pulls him forward and
downward...which action leaves the man speechless
and only able to clutch Alf's wrist.
 Heidi has her berretta pointing at the other men.
 Seven walks to the side, and stays near them.

Alf (brings Dahal to the table)-
 Draw your weapon! Put it on the table!
Mr. Dahal (puts his pistol on the table)-
 I don't know you!
 (speaks to the Nepali man)
 Bring us tea!
Heidi (to the other men)-
 Drop your pistols onto the ground!
 (they do that)
 Sit at the table!
 (they sit)

 There is movement at the northwest corner, as two

thin and bent village men enter, followed by Mr. Kuerile and Indu.

Mr. Kuerile stops at the entrance and waits. He is soon joined by two men, one apparently a newsman, with packsack and microphone, and the other a man who is considered worthy of being questioned.

As they enter, so does a large number of youthful men and women in uniform, in three units of ten each, that come to a position before the buildings.

The three men go directly to the table.

Mr. Kuerile (offers his hand to Alf)-
    Mr. Alf...this is a great Maoist leader...in all Nepal. Mr. K.B. Mahada.

Mr. Mahada appears to be in his middle thirties, is of average height, and stocky. He has a relaxed and agreeable manner. His right hand now goes forward a few inches toward Alf...and Alf responds.

They shake hands.

Newsman-
    Is it all right to have the interview now? I must get to Jiri soon...and Kathmandu...to send my story.
Mr. Mahada (to Mr. Kuerile and Alf)-
    This is CNN news. Mr. Bindara. I invited him to this, knowing he wouldn't disclose our location.
Bindara (holds forward the microphone)-
    You stand at the doorstep of peace talks...and will be one of those at the table...Mr. Mahada.
    The government of Nepal has called you terrorist, and put a price tag of sixty five thousand dollars on

your head.

Mahada-

The Nepali people are with us. We are a political force and do not support terrorism...which is what a few people do for their own selfish reason.

Bindara-

You have strikes, across Nepal...the cessation of work and other movement...and if the people don't obey they are killed in cold blood. These are called terrorist acts.

Mahada-

Baseless allegations made by the government. We don't kill civilians. The Nepalese government is responsible for that. They kill innocent people who support our cause. Such as this...that seven people were killed in Kabri District which the government called Maoists but they had no weapons, they were just innocent musicians.

At Salan, innocent people were killed in an air raid by the government...at a fair...and they called them Maoists. The government claims to have killed four thousand Maoists...but where are the arms or the uniforms recovered from them? Our fighters wear uniforms. Why doesn't the government show them?

Bindara-

Are you aware that most nations are agreeing to call you terrorists?

Mahada-

Yes! Also, that Amnesty International reported human rights abuses by the government.

(takes a paper from his jacket's inner pocket and reads from it)

"Many of those unlawfully killed by the Security Force were civilians targeted for their real or perceived support for Maoist rebels".

And the report said other deaths were Maoists deliberately killed by the Security Force after being arrested.

Bindara-

Are you angry that the world does not seem to understand the nature of your cause?

Mahada-

The rulers of today's world often make wrong decisions related to their conflict with terror...and forget about justified revolution.

Bindara-

You have said this fight is not your wish.

Mahada-

It is the ruling class that has committed injustice for many years. They must want this to end...with their acceptance of that truth.

Bindara-

This fighting...has been six years. Why is there no peace?

Mahada-

When the ruling class empowers all people with the right to vote, peace will prevail.

The government must decentralize their power to the people of this nation. The King must give up his powers.

Bindara-

Why do the rulers...the King in particular...avoid having constituent assembly, to allow voting for all?

Mahada-

If voting occurs...for all...the people will win. The King and many corrupt high-cast Hindus will be gone. The common man is against them.

Bindara-

Isn't it also true that many high-caste Hindus are against corruption?

Mahada-

Thanks for saying that. Many in Parliament are not corrupt.

(he looks around, then shouts)

This will be our last war. The government has received outside help to crush innocent people, but the people will win.

This war is legal...according to a natural right to end oppression.

Alf (in a strong voice)-

As an American I agree...that all who wish to have a life of equality...have a right to revolution. But...as you know, there are some with no uniforms who rob from the people. Such a group came through here yesterday.

Mr. Kuerile-

Yes...I told Mr. Mahada of that.

Alf (points to Dahal and his men)-

And there are some who do not rob, but plot blindly against the King...so that violence may kill those in the way, even at a fair, or a corner of the street near the palace.

Dahal (leaps to his feet)-

I was robbed last night by that other army. I'm not like them. But we must put terror and death into

the government. It's the only way to victory.
Mahada-
    If we lack sufficient military power, the instilling
of fear will not serve hope. Now...restraint is best.

A new voice enters. Everyone listens.

Seven (yet dressed as a Brahmin)-
    Desperation breeds brutality. In Nepal...fear has
increased in the people. They ask "Have Maoists
made life better?" Even when the government kills
the innocent, it is often perceived that this terror
is brought by revolution that has gone on too long.
    You must, once again, go to the peace table.
Dahal-
    This is insanity! The King's Army now has M-16
rifles supplied by America...and sub-machine guns
from Belgium.
Mahada-
    Also...they have orders to cease fire. A truce has
been called. I will be a negotiator.
Bindara-
    Do you think the government will set up proper
atmosphere for talks? In Kathmandu...for two days
now, some ministers have set demands, and told
their audience that almost nothing will change of
the Hindu system, or with the King's paternal grip.
Mahada-
    Who controls the Nepali Army?
    (to the entire audience)
    Who dissolved Parliament, without constitutional
authority?

Bindara-

The King did! He is now in India for a visit.

Mahada-

And yet he must admit change…and give up his power to all the people, as they determine the face of Parliament.

Now…he controls the army. Power is his. But even most of his followers want peace talks.

Bindara-

Some…in Parliament say the King has no need to be present.

Mahada-

They want things to stay as they are. Greed and privilege hide the point…that the King's rule must end. He is the center of corruption and inequality.

Mr. Kuerile-

The King is the top of caste. I'm in dirt earning the price of a tea bag. The armless and legless beg.

It is not any God who keeps people in the dirt. If peace talks fail to make changes, I might agree to kill. Yes…many toimes.

Mahada-

With both sides at a table, perhaps we can put the King aside. We can transfer authority to those who want an election watched over by the international community.

This means the Nepali Army must leave the King's hands.

(he walks several feet, to face his army)

We have been the People's Army. We have fought with courage. And the day will come when all Nepal will be free of corruption.

From this army a great shout arises...and, as one, all weapons are held overhead. A young woman, with a red bandana around her neck, steps forward.

Young woman-
    We will prevail! Freedom and equality belong to all!

A young Nepali man runs from the northwest corner of the town, and comes to the center.

Young Nepali man (shouts)-
    The band of robbers is here. They have returned.

Mahada directs his army to retreat to the buildings, to hide behind them. He goes with them, as does Bindara.
    On a building's porch are the old man and woman, the two thin Nepali men, and Indu with her child.
    At the center stands Alf, Heidi, and Seven. Dahal and his men are seated at the table.
    The band of robbers enters...then they walk to the center.

Robber leader (smiles at Alf)-
    You and your wife will give us ninety U.S. dollars.
Alf-
    You don't have the sense you were born with!
Dahal (leaps to his feet)-
    I was on the bus you robbed!
Robber leader (points his rifle at Dahal)-
    Where is Mr. Kuerile? Did he go to the river...and

not yet return?

Mahada and Mr. Kuerile enter, followed by the army, which seems to come in from everywhere.

Mahada (to robber leader)-
    Put all your weapons on the table.

This is done in silence, after which the robbers stand as before.

Dahal-
    He has my money and watch...and theirs,
    (points at his four companions)
    Also...of the people on the bus.
    (steps toward the robbers)
    How much more?
Mahada-
    Wait!

Dahal stops.

Mahada (to the robbers)-
    Take off all clothing...except underwear. Put any jewelry you have...on the table.
    (motions to the girl with the red bandana, for her to come to him. Also, he calls in a uniformed man who was apart yet very near the lines of the army)
Robber leader (wearing only underwear)-
    But this is my necklace. It was my wife's.
Mahada-
    Put it on the table.

(speaks to the uniformed man he called in)
Sergeant...you and my daughter empty their
pockets...then give the clothing back.

This is done. Then the robbers put on their clothes.

Mahada (inspects what is on the table)-
How many of us have stolen from ordinary
citizens...even from the hungry? How many of us
are murderers? And do any of us smile at the next
victim and the next?
Put on your wife's necklace!

The robber leader puts on his wife's necklace.

Mahada-
Sergeant, you and four others take these men
down the trail, to the northwest, until you find a
place by the river. Shoot them! Then do their souls
an honor we shouldn't deny...in our little human
judgment. Cremate them and put some ashes of
each into the river...which river is flowing toward
the heart of Nepal.

The sergeant and four other men direct the robbers
to the northwest trail, and disappear.

Bindara-
Mr. Mahada...why do you send them to the heart of
Nepal?
Mahada-
It was in my heart to do it...for the innocence in

the robbers.
Bindara-
   But...perhaps God will deny them that dignity.
Seven (yet as a Brahmin)-
   God has shown man's central innocence...by the
   fact that he exists. Whatever goodness is hidden,
   existence is every man's dignity. This is the nature
   of compassion.
Mahada-
   The robbers and murderers, for what they did,
   deserve to die. But...because the soul of each is
   innocent within, our punishment must have dignity.
   Also...Mr. Kuerile's child ought not to believe he is
   born to be spit at, or that he defiles a cup of tea if
   he touches it on the way to a higher caste person.
   If the King and governers can't see this...I, too,
   may become brutal.
   We must leave. I will go to Kathmandu.
Bindara-
   What of your army?
Mahada-
   They will hide in the shadows of the night.
   Mr. Kuerile...do you have rice to spare? Or, did the
   Robbers take it all? What else did they take?
Mr. Kuerile-
   They took much of our rice...and they killed my
   daughter's husband, Raju, because he refused to
   join them. But we have some rice...for you.
   Also, I have explosives. My daughter, Indu, will
   take the girl with the red bandana to them.
Mahada-
   Keep your rice, my friend. One of my army will

buy some later. Tomorrow a car will come to Jiri,
to take me away for peace talks in Kathmandu.

Are the explosives well hidden? If I should need
some, later, will it be safe until then?
Mr. Kuerile-

Yes, I'll keep some for you. No amount of search
would find it. But I will tell you...now...where it is.
(he gets close to Mahada, and whispers)
Mahada (raises his head)-

The King's Army is searching for the robbers. If
they surprise us here, and have M-16s, many of us
will die...including those of you who call this home.
Bindara-

That army would kill you? What of the truce?
Mahada-

The King's Army might be willing to ignore it.
Seven-

They would violate international law. If death is
dealt by the King's Army, your right to revolution
would be carried sadly in the wind.
Alf-

Mr. Mahada...we agree with your decision to go
forward peacefully. Or, at least, try for that.
Mahada-

That you and the Brahmin sound alike...is matter
for another day.

Why have you given Israel billions and only a few
dollar's worth to Palestine, whose territory is
bullied with the houses of Israel, as they build new
ones and promise again and again to depart?
Alf-

A major part of the world's tenor is "I am better

than you". When that is part of religious doctrine
it can seem to be certified. Sometimes we forget
that all men are created equal.
Mahada (rubs his eyes)-
    I once saw your movie..."Singing in the Rain". My
daughter wants to do that.

The girl with the red bandana, and Indu, and two
young men bring to the table several bags of rice,
and a basket containing three chickens.

Mahada-
    We choose to leave that...but thank you.
Indu-
    I will join you...and bring my boy to Jiri. My father
will get him when he passes through.
    (goes to her father, and hugs him)
Bindara-
    I must depart...to catch my flight from Jiri.

After Bindara bows, he puts his hands together and
against his forehead...then walks to the boulders at
the south side, and disappears.

Girl with the red bandana-
    Father...you seem weary. There is a place along
the trail, by the river, where travelers stop to rest.
Indu has told me of it.
Mr. Kuerile-
    Depart from behind my house, and climb the hill.
And...soon...we'll see you in the apple orchard.
Can you see it?
    (points upward, to the east)

Then...in a half hour you will be down to the river. There is a small crossing.

Mahada shakes hands with Mr. Kuerile, and with Alf and Heidi. To Seven, he bows...hands together quite high.
He faces Dahal.

Mahada-
Put aside excess. There will be more M-16s.
Dahal (standing)-
One day you might be brutal.
Mahada-
If so...it would ease the pain where love once dreamed. And now...I pray for the love of all.
Goodbye my friends. Mr. Kuerile, please tell the sergeant where this army has gone.

Mahada and his army soon disappear behind Mr. Kuerile's building.

Mr. Kuerile-
This town has died. A blind man would know, hearing only what is at this table.
Alf-
Mr. Kuerile...I know of a place where deaf people sing...and being loved...are where they once belonged. And sing again...and again.
One day this fighting will end...and changes will occur. You can own this land, and be at your table.
Heidi-
The old man and woman are here, and those two

thin village men. Has work aged them so?

    Where is the young lady with the baby?

Mr. Kuerile-

    I think she went away.

    (shouts toward the buildings)

    Old woman! Tell your daughter to get to Jiri!

    (to Heidi)

    All gone! And I will be to Kathmandu to seek work.
If Raju lived...I might have brought all my children
here.

Heidi-

    But you can return some day. And all the others.

Mr. Kuerile-

    Nothing here belongs to us.

    (faces Alf)

    My friend...sometimes patience dies.

Heidi-

    Where you gather...love belongs to you. And then
one day...

Mr. Kuerile-

    Today...is a sadness. The ground, the buildings,
and this table...yes, even the apple orchard there
above...belong to Bahadur Pun, of Kathmandu.

    The privileged can sell the shit for fertilizer. I am
the shit.

Alf-

    You will find a place to love...where all are equal.

Heidi (points up the hill)-

    There they are...in the apple orchard. I can see
the girl with the red bandana.

    (steps to Alf)

    She's gone.

Alf-
   Mr. Kuerile...the King's Army, in Jiri, would have
been alerted last night about the bus robbery.
Mr. Kuerile-
   I'll take these weapons into the trees. Here is a
pistol I like.
   (he reaches to the table)
   But...I can't have it. On the way to Kathmandu, the
police would arrest me.
Dahal-
   That's my pistol!
   (holds out his hand)

   Mr. Kuerile puts the pistol into Dahal's hand, and
motions for Dahal's men to retrieve their weapons.

Mr. Kuerile-
   What remains of weapons...I'll take to the hillside.
The jewelry and watches to the police station in
Jiri,
Dahal (holds his pistol high, and looks at it)-
   What have you done with Raju's money?

   Mr. Kuerile is so angered by this question, his anger
is obvious, although he doesn't speak. He looks
upward, and raises his hands, clenched into fists.
Then...yet looking upward, he opens them.

Dahal-
   Also...where are the explosives? I can shoot you!
Alf-
   But you won't! You feel my pistol at your belly!

Dahal drops the gun to the ground.

Heidi, with hers drawn, directs the other men to
stand away from the table.

Seven gets Dahal's pistol and puts it into a burlap
sack, along with all other weapons on the table.

Seven (points to the northwest corner)-
    Get out! But it's not for me to say. Mr. Kuerile...?
Mr. Kuerile-
    Even now this is my home...and most men can
    climb to it. But those full of themselves...have no
    room for air in the higher places. Yes...get out!

The group walks away a few steps, then Dahal
stops to speak.

Dahal (to Alf)-
    I know you're an American. This is my country!
Seven-
    But she doesn't belong to you...you belong to her.
    She feels your treachery, as time goes by.

Dahal and his men walk to the northwest corner,
and disappear from sight.

Mr. Kuerile (shouts at the building to the north)-
    Mrs. Mandahar...will you please make tea for us.

There is no response from inside the buildings.

Alf-
    Mr. Kuerile, if Dahal comes here after you're gone,

could he find the explosives?

Mr. Kuerile-

No! I buried them under this table. Then I dug a ditch to that building where the old man and woman lived with my daughter and her baby. I put wires in the ditch. In the kitchen is a board three feet long that comes up, and if you reach down at the center of it and ten inches to the left, you can dig up the ends of the wiring. Nearby...across the room...is a battery.

Alf-

And this table would blow skyward.

Mr. Kuerile-

Yes. But at the water tub, here, rest eight sticks of dynamite which are half buried. Easy to find. I fastened wire to them, connected to nothing.

Alf-

And whoever finds it will think that's all of it.

Mr. Kuerile (laughs)-

I worked through the evening to carry out this plan.

(again he shouts for the elders...in vain)

Would I connect wire ends to a battery...truly?

(he sighs)

Now it is time for me to get these weapons to the hillside. Then I'll take the jewelry and watches to Jiri...and myself to Kathmandu.

Mahada's sergeant and his two young assistants appear at the northwest corner, and move toward the center. He greets them all with a nod, and shakes hands with Mr. Kuerile.

Mr. Kuerile-
   I told my lookout to announce everyone. Did you
   see Mr. Dahal and his men?
Sergeant-
   Yes. They hid beside the trail as we passed, then I
   watched them move away...downward.
Mr. Kuerile-
   I have sticks of dynamite in that packsack. To be
   Buried. You are welcome to take some.
Sergeant-
   I don't want it. Mr. Mahada will go to peace talks,
   and my hope is strong that changes will come.
Mr. Kuerile (shouts)-
   Old woman! Get tea, please!
Seven (looks at his watch)-
   To catch the plane...it's time to leave. No eleven
   hour bus ride for me.
Alf-
   Yes. Goodbye, Mr. Kuerile.
   (they shake hands)
   And sergeant...good luck to you and your people.
Alf (shakes hands, around)-
   Mr. Kuerile...I'll visit you in Kathmandu next year,
   or the next. And Heidi will come, too...perhaps.
Heidi-
   Probably.

Alf, Heidi, and Seven move toward the south edge,
and the two boulders. They stop, and look back.

Mr. Kuerile (shouts)-
   Are you one family?

Heidi (points at Seven_
     I call him Dad.
Mr. Kuerile-
     You must remember this...my home is all Nepal.
     Please come again...to see me in it.

     Mr. Kuerile waves, as does the sergeant and his
men, then he reaches into one of his packs and pulls
out a stick of dynamite. He moves it through the air
above him.
     He is smiling broadly.
     Now he brings his arm down to his side and, yet
smiling, shakes his head.

Heidi-
     He wonders what to do with it?
Alf-
     Yes. Also..."Should I laugh...or should I cry?"

     A rifle shot rings out...and Mr. Kuerile falls.
     The sergeant and his men jerk their heads toward
the west edge where the trees rest on the slight rise.
And...that's all the time they have because, now,
many gun shots cut through the day.
     A long silence comes.
     Everyone at the center is dead.
     Eight of the King's Army walk from the trees.

     Both Alf and Heidi draw their weapons.

Heidi-
     They murdered them!

Seven (grasps her shoulder)-

    Wait!..daughter. Alf...be still!

Heidi-

    They broke the truce!

Seven-

    Holster your gun! You, too, Alf!

Alf-

    And yet...I must respond to that.

Seven-

    No! We won't rush in to call them what they're not.

Heidi-

    Not murderers? Dad, where are your tears?

    Seven pulls Alf and Heidi closer to a boulder, to be hidden.

Seven-

    Tell her what the soldiers are, Alf.

Alf (sighs, then speaks strongly)-

    Ignorant! Perhaps thinking they had the robbers. But maybe worse than that? Did they come to the edge and, after seeing armed men, decide to kill... not giving a damn who they were?

    They ought to be punished?

Seven-

    I'll see to it, Alf. They'll be punished!

Alf-

    Shouldn't I care enough about my friend, to be a fool...and rush in? I might get all those so-called innocent bastards.

Seven-

    The soldiers are human...with the usual capacity

to be stupid. Equality...the truth of what they're made of...the stuff of the stars...is hidden in the mist. And far from the inner clarity, poor thought has made inequality the center of ignorance.

In Jiri, I'll make certain that Mr. Kuerile and the others are cremated. And I'll report the breaking of the truce, by way of brutality. Be patient! Happy existence proves equality...but proof counts for little before the dust settles.

Alf-
  For Mr. Kuerile...patience was a lot of dust.

Heidi (sighs...and leans against Alf)-
  Mr. Kuerile had a rainbow. He was in it with his children.

Alf (puts his arm around her)-
  Sure!

Heidi-
  And they sang to one another...always.

Alf-
  Even through the night!

Seven-
  Daughter...son...it's time to go!

  The three turn away.
  The boulders are rolled back into place.

(Back cover)

After long oppression...begins the fight for equality. The oppressor becomes brutal. Some revolutionaries match the brutality...to be rid of it.

The world calls you terrorist and gives money and guns to the oppressor.

You laugh and cry at the same time.

You try to love what you hate.

And, with the dignity of existence, you remain willing to fight for freedom...against all odds.

* * *

Alf Whitmore has been hired to observe a man who sells explosives. He follows him to Alaska, China, and Nepal. In Nepal he sees the face of revolution.